BECOMING

Beauty

Praise for *Becoming Beauty*

"It's hard to believe this is Boucher's first novel. The writing is sophisticated and striking, and the story captivating. It immediately pulls the reader into the clutches of its charm. *Becoming Beauty* is a much welcome addition to the genre."
—MELISSA LEMON, author of *Snow Whyte and the Queen of Mayhem* and *Cinder and Ella*

"A refreshing twist on Beauty and the Beast where beauty is more than skin deep."
—JANICE SPERRY, author of *The Rebel Princess*

"An unexpected twist on a traditional fairy tale. Boucher has created a flawed heroine you'll love, and a hero that isn't what you expect. Prepare to be enchanted by this debut novel from a promising new author. I look forward to what she comes up with next!"
—CINDY C. BENNETT, author of *Geek Girl* and *Rapunzel Untangled*

"Intriguing and charming, complete with character transformations befitting a twist on the classic Beauty and the Beast."
—LAUREN SKIDMORE, author of *What is Hidden*

BECOMING
Beauty

SARAH E. BOUCHER

SWEETWATER
BOOKS

AN IMPRINT OF CEDAR FORT, INC.
SPRINGVILLE, UTAH

This is a work of fiction. The characters, names, incidents, places, and dialogue are products of the author's imagination, and are not to be construed as real. The opinions and views expressed herein belong solely to the author and do not necessarily represent the opinions or views of Cedar Fort, Inc. Permission for the use of sources, graphics, and photos is also solely the responsibility of the author.

ISBN 13: 978-1-4621-1455-9

Published by Sweetwater Books, an imprint of Cedar Fort, Inc.
2373 W. 700 S., Springville, UT 84663
Distributed by Cedar Fort, Inc., www.cedarfort.com

LIBRARY OF CONGRESS CATALOGING-IN-PUBLICATION DATA

Boucher, Sarah E., 1976- author.
Becoming Beauty : a retelling of Beauty and the Beast / Sarah E. Boucher.
    pages cm
Summary: Obsessed with landing a wealthy nobleman and escaping her humdrum life, Bella instead finds herself the captive of a man-like Beast whose repellent presence is only made bearable by Jack, the Beast's sole companion.
ISBN 978-1-4621-1455-9 (perfect : alk. paper)
[1. Fairy tales. 2. Monsters--Fiction. 3. Love--Fiction.] I. Title.
PZ8.B64435Be 2014
[Fic]--dc23
                                2014013415

Cover design by Kristen Reeves
Cover design © 2014 by Lyle Mortimer
Edited by Melissa J. Caldwell and Daniel Friend
Typeset by Melissa J. Caldwell

Printed in the United States of America

10 9 8 7 6 5 4 3 2 1

For Mom, who introduced me to fairy tales,
and Dad, who taught me to love big words.

One

*W*eaving a trail of well-bred chatter across the ballroom, ladies of wealth and status bustled past me, their expensive gowns swishing as they hurried toward their next conquests. Compared to the brightness of the company, the tall, heavily draped windows were somber, even with candlelight flickering from the sconces lining the walls. The carefully glossed floor shimmered; however, under so many dancing slippers and burnished knee boots, a number of small tables set around the perimeter of the room, and the long, linen-draped buffet table laden with every delicacy imaginable, the floor itself was barely visible.

Having just entered the room, I scanned the assembly for persons of interest. The regular crowd was performing the polite, monotonous dance of courtship. Then there he was, standing out like a diamond in a handful of pebbles—and seemingly all alone. Dressed as a nobleman, he sported a starched cravat twisted into the latest fashion, boots that gleamed like freshly polished onyx, and the best-tailored jacket of anyone in the room.

Mr. Mason.

His name flitted about the room in hushed whispers and covert glances. Since this would be my last ball for a time, Mr. Mason's appearance was positively providential.

I observed lady after lady approaching him, only to be rebuffed. How could they be so blind? Even from across the room, I could tell he lived for the thrill of the hunt. A true hunter never wants his prey to lumber up to him, serve itself up, and beg to be devoured. No, the true hunter selects and stalks his prey, and after much deliberation, chooses the moment of attack.

A tiny smile curved my lips. This would be easy, not to mention entertaining.

"Mr. Dawlish," I said, sidling up to Mr. Mason and looping a hand through his elbow, "I believe this is our—" I gasped, released his elbow, and, making my eyes as large as I could, sank into a deep curtsy, murmuring a breathless, "Pardon me, sir."

Through my eyelashes, I saw Mr. Mason look me up and down, his eyes dwelling a second longer on the neckline of my gown and the pearls at my throat.

"It's perfectly all right, my dear," he said in a low tone.

I relaxed my face and reiterated, "I really must beg your pardon, sir. I seem to have confused you with my dance partner." I glanced about in search of the fictional Mr. Dawlish and added, "Who seems to be missing at the moment."

"Perhaps I can be of assistance." He pulled himself up

to his full height, a good two handspans taller than me. "Might I stand in for the absent Mr. Dawlish?"

"Oh, no," I replied, sounding flustered. "What if he returns and finds me dancing with another? No, it would be entirely improper." Settling my lips into a line, I added, "In fact, I should go find him. I thank you for your kindness." Bobbing a quick curtsey, I made as if to leave.

He put his hand on my arm, stopping me. "I insist. After all, what sort of man arranges for a dance with a young woman and then disappears? Now *that*, my dear, is true impropriety. Should Mr. Dawlish return, he shall have me to reckon with." And before you could say, *Mr. Dawlish is a sham*, he had whisked me into the middle of the dance floor.

Everything was going according to plan. In no time, I had secured the most eligible bachelor, and with any luck—after a suitable courtship—he'd be asking for my hand in marriage and making me the mistress of what-ever beautiful place he called home. Our balls, dinner parties, and afternoon soirees would put this one to shame. As long as I could keep my home life a secret— at least until he was sufficiently smitten—everything would work out.

Mr. Mason's warm hand pressed to the small of my back, the other cradling my right hand and anchoring me to the center of the ballroom. With the chandelier overhead bathing us in golden light and the room and its occupants spinning around me like puppets bowing and dancing at the master's whim, I felt as powerful as a monarch. All of it, from my well-dressed partner to the young ladies casting me envious looks, carried the same message: tonight was my night.

Perhaps if the women had learned something from our time attending balls together, they could have been dancing with the most attractive man in the room instead of glaring menacingly at me. After all, we had been occupying the sole ballroom in Stanton since each of us had become "eligible"—that time between girlhood and womanhood when a lady does all in her power to ensure a good match before being relegated to spinsterhood. If they had spent less time giving me the evil eye and more time studying my technique, they wouldn't be facing this dilemma.

I ignored them and basked in the glow of my partner's dark eyes. Who cared that I didn't have as much money as three-quarters of the ladies in attendance? I possessed something they didn't, and it was that special something that had landed me in this man's arms.

Pasting on my most demure expression, I looked up at him, prepared to set him on the track to the altar. But instead of looking at me, instead of admiring my lovely form and myriad charms, he was staring over my shoulder.

"Mr. Mason? Are you quite all right?" I hoped against hope that he wasn't looking where I imagined he was, but the telltale gleam in his eyes was unmistakable. If I could just make him look at me . . .

"What, my dear?" His eyes, soft and dreamy, met my gaze. He blinked and then blinked again. "Oh—I'm quite sorry. I seem to have forgotten that this dance was spoken for." Swiftly, he moved me off the dance floor and back to the line of waiting wallflowers. "After all, I'm sure Mr. Dawlish will have returned by now."

"Wait—" I attempted, but he was already gone. I didn't want to watch him go or to see who had diverted his attention. My stomach twisted with a mixture of anger and frustration as I turned to face the broad entryway. Even the best of feminine wiles—mine, for instance— were useless when Beauty Incarnate stepped into the room. Her face, framed by hair the color of polished gold and allegedly carved by angels, drew every masculine eye. Her admirers, acutely aware of her flawless figure and fine features, never noticed that the dress and slippers were the same ones she donned at every ball. She wore no other adornment. She didn't need to.

The other women in the room should have reacted like a den of cats whose sole tom had been whisked out from under their noses. But Cassandra's sweet disposition ensured that she was well-respected. Only I, who knew her best, saw and enumerated her flaws.

After all, she was my sister.

Surely someone else had noticed the out-of-fashion dress and lack of jewelry. Perhaps I should use my powers of persuasion on the ladies in the room, just so I'd have someone with whom to commiserate. Glancing around, I saw them grouped in twos or threes and gossiping just as they had been before my sister's arrival. What good would it do me to go to the effort of befriending them? I had no use for idle tittle-tattle, and the ladies could offer nothing to better my family's financial situation.

Narrowing my gaze, I refocused on the root of my problem: Cassandra. What if I launched a beaded slipper at her head? It wouldn't cause any lasting damage, I reasoned. The crowd of men would be gathered about her, eager to catch her every word, and then *WHAP!* Looks of stunned outrage would paint their faces as she fell in a graceless heap at their feet.

I savored the image, letting it linger in my mind far longer than I should have before releasing it with a sigh. One wasn't permitted to harm one's own sister, not with a dancing slipper anyway, and certainly not in the middle of a ball. There were far too many witnesses.

I groaned inwardly. It really wasn't her fault. She hadn't asked to be born with such beauty. In fact, it may have suited her better to be as plain as I was. But that was the way of it. Beauty, like youth and wealth, was wasted on the wrong people.

As gentleman after gentleman strode up to Cassandra to escort her to the dance floor, I did my best to keep my chin up. Beside her, I felt as out of place as a cabbage leaf blown into a rose bed. I comforted myself that although my face and form weren't as lovely as hers, they were offset by the costly string of pearls at my throat and a gown ten times finer than hers.

Courtship was like war: if you wanted to win, you dressed for it. In place of bucklers and shields, swords and protective armor, women donned dresses designed to catch the eye and dancing shoes their fathers could barely afford. A woman couldn't help being born to a working-class carpenter, but that didn't mean she had to accept fate and settle down to a life of monotony and too many children. With the right accoutrements and a fair bit of cleverness, a girl like me could win her place by the side of someone like Mr. Mason.

Yet regardless of my careful planning and beautiful clothing, there he was, at Cassie's side instead of mine.

It's not as if this hasn't happened before, an inner voice whispered. Like so many others who had been drawn in by my impressive array of fine clothing, Mr. Mason had chosen my sister over me in the end. *This gown is a victory in itself*, I comforted myself, pushing the other thought to the back of my mind. Running my hands over the sapphire-blue fabric, I luxuriated in the tightness of the bodice, the bell of the skirt, and the intricate beading edging the sleeves and hem. With a grin of satisfaction, I recalled the conversation that led to its acquisition.

"Daddy, there's a dance coming up," I had cooed sweetly, looping an arm around the back of his worn easy chair and treating him to my most winning smile. The "now what?" expression was already forming in his gray-green eyes.

"It will be the event of the season—ladies in gorgeous dresses and gentlemen in their finery."

From the tight line of his mouth and the concern wrinkling his brow, I could tell he was already on the defensive. When he spoke, his words were stiff. "Bella, darling, you already have many beautiful clothes."

"True. You have been kind enough to provide the best for me." We both knew this was a lie; even the most humble hatpin didn't come without a fight. "Even though I'm not pretty like Cassie or brilliant like Aaron." Emphasizing my siblings' gifts made mine look paltry in comparison. Pity was the best tool when dealing with Father.

"They also work, my dear," he said, "to provide for themselves. Not only is Cass beautiful, but she is also skilled and weaves fabric to sell. And you know Aaron's inventions are in high demand." He didn't spell it out, but the implication was there: I toiled not, neither did I spin, but I expected to be arrayed in the best even though his income could ill afford it.

"Exactly, Father." I nodded, lulling him into a false sense of security. "They possess such impressive skills. What have I to offer?"

I perceived that he was beginning to weaken; the furrows around his mouth and eyes were softening. The next step was a swift blow to the heart. "If Mother had been around longer," I began, "I could have learned a more profitable skill from her. Cooking or cleaning . . ." My voice trailed off. A single tear trickled down my cheek.

The dress and shoes were as good as mine.

His whole frame slumped in the chair, looking as old and shabby as the sparsely furnished room he inhabited. His voice was sorrowful when he finally said, "I regret that you did not know her. She was a wonderful mother, the best of women . . ." He fell silent for a moment, running a lined hand through his graying hair. I knew he was thinking about how much he loved and missed her, how after more than fifteen years he still did not have room in his heart for another. "I cannot provide a mother for you, child, but I can provide this. Go and choose whatever you want. It is yours." I embraced him then, playing the part of the grateful daughter. Outwardly, I rambled excitedly about the upcoming event. Inwardly, I gloated over my conquest.

I twitched my blue skirts into place with a deep sense of satisfaction. The moment I had seen this gown in the shop window—coveted by every girl who passed by—I knew it would be worth the battle. Given that half the eligible women my age were better looking and had substantial dowries to offer their prospective companions, my chances of capturing a man's fancy were slim. The gift of fine clothes, shoes, and jewelry improved my chances, even if it intensified the other ladies' dislike for me. My impeccable taste paired with a certain ruthlessness had that effect on them. Their outright hostility generally worked in my favor. Paired with my finery, it was enough to make most men sit up and take notice— when they weren't panting after Cassie, that is.

"Pardon me, miss. Would you care to dance?"

It would have been luck indeed if Mr. Mason had suffered an attack of conscience. He was one of the few in attendance who knew nothing about the less-than-ideal circumstances of my family, and capturing his fancy would have made my last ball a success. But, of course, it wasn't Mr. Mason. Instead, when I turned around, a nervous young man stood before me.

Judging from his plain but serviceable brown suit and simply tied neckcloth, he was probably a second or third son. He couldn't have been from Stanton; he must have hailed from one of the smaller communities—like mine—that skirted the city. No matter. Not one to discourage an eligible gentleman, I bowed my acceptance, donned a demure smile, and offered him my hand. The music started as we settled into place on the dance floor, clasped hands, and began the steps. I schooled my expression into one of humble sweetness—patterned after Cassie—and focused the full strength of it on my partner. The effort was lost on him; like Mr. Mason, his eyes were fixed firmly over my shoulder. My lips drew into a line as I followed his gaze and found it centered on my sister.

Really, one slight was quite enough. Twice was intolerable.

"Lovely, isn't she?" I commented, covering the venom in my voice with a tone of politeness.

"She's an angel," he replied. Then, realizing what he'd said, he refocused on me. Eyes filled with panic, he attempted to retract the statement. "I mean, *you* are as lovely as an angel, Miss . . . uh . . ."

"Bella," I replied with what I hoped was an amiable grin. "It means 'beautiful.' But I can't fault you for admiring my sister. Everyone does."

Naturally, he rose to the bait. "Your sister?" His eyes flicked from Cassie to me, trying to catch some similarity between us. "Pardon me for saying so, but you look nothing alike." He phrased the comment kindly, but I could read the meaning in his eyes. Everyone drew comparisons between Cassandra and me, and I always came out lacking.

It made no real difference in this case anyway. His fixation with Cassie was vexing, but as a second son, he didn't have the power to help me escape the humble life I led. As far as I was concerned, Cass or any other woman in the room was welcome to him.

That didn't mean I wouldn't make him pay for his inattention.

Quirking an eyebrow, I quipped, "Cassandra's ethereal beauty as opposed to . . . ?"

A muscle in his cheek twitched as he tried to come up with a complimentary description—something which wouldn't result in his toes getting flattened by my heel. "Your comeliness?" His face paled.

Concerned with making the right impression on the other gentlemen in the room, I only wanted to make him squirm for a moment. His toes had never been in any real danger. Dropping my lashes, I emitted a girlish giggle. "Such flattery!"

Pleased at having placated me so easily, he relaxed into a smile.

Perhaps I should step on his toes after all.

Hours later, in the privacy of Cassandra's and my bedroom, I slid my feet from my beaded slippers and rubbed them to restore circulation. My dancing shoes hadn't been selected for comfort, and they pinched badly. Add to that the scores of graceless youths who had trod upon my feet while getting a closer look at my sister, and my poor toes had suffered indeed. I had hoped that when I turned twenty, Father would allow me to attend social events unescorted, but either from an outdated sense of propriety or to encourage Cassie to select a suitor, he stood resolute. No matter. Father would be leaving on an extended business trip soon and I would have my chance to escape his watchful eye.

"Did they step on your feet again?" Cassie inquired, sympathy flavoring her voice as she, too, removed her ball gown and slippers.

"While craning their necks to get a better look at you, you mean?" I replied, still rubbing at my aching toes.

Cassie sighed. "I don't understand why Father insists I attend these things."

"Perhaps he'd like to see you married," I suggested flatly.

Her eyes, no less bright after the exertions of the evening, met mine. "He means well, but I'm sure you'd have a much better time without me. And you know I'd prefer to stay home."

There was the painful truth. My sister, who could have any marriageable man, preferred the home she grew up in and the company of her kin. I, who hated our home and longed for a place in society, repeatedly failed to attract a suitable prospect.

"I'll speak with him again and ask him to reconsider allowing you to go without me," Cassie said. "Maybe Aaron can serve as your escort." The thought of my younger brother being forced to attend the various balls and soirees that Cassie and I frequented was unimaginable. Aaron's only joy in life lay in tinkering with bits of this or that. He had little use for Stanton society.

Helping me out of my dress and into my nightgown, Cassie assured me, "I'll speak with Father as soon as he returns from his trip. I'm certain I can make him see sense this time. Clearly, you value these things more than I do." She snuffed out the light, bid me good night, and climbed into her bed.

Lying in my own cot, waiting for sleep to come, I pondered her last words with a mixture of anger and frustration. She had repeatedly gotten between me and eligible gentlemen, but no more. She had no idea how I valued society functions or what I would do to achieve all I had set my sights on. Neither Cassie, my lack of funds, nor Father's archaic beliefs would stand between me and the brilliant match that would ensure the life of luxury I was born to live.

Two

The day dawned bright and clear, only a faint breeze shushing through the eaves. The long-coveted blue gown hung over the end of my bed, testament to the festivities of the night before. I fingered the beaded sleeves while Cassie headed toward the main room of our home. Why did it have to be the last ball? Couldn't Father have postponed his trip? The naïve part of me wanted to question why I had to forego certain entertainments to accommodate his travel, but a carpenter's daughter knows how scarce work can be at times. Without regular employment, the family would move from respectable working-class to poverty in a matter of months. Father's superior craftsmanship was well known and highly valued, and a nobleman from Camdon had sent for him—promising generous compensation not only for the work, but also for the time and travel required. My father could not miss the opportunity to better our family's situation.

"Cassie?" I called.

She retraced her steps until she was standing in the doorway. "Yes?"

"I wish he didn't have to go."

A sad smile crossed her face. "Me too, Bella."

Subdued, we made our way to the main room, where Father waited to bid us farewell.

The horse had been readied, Father's tools and provisions packed carefully into saddlebags. The journey to Camdon and back would take the better part of a month, with another month to complete the work. It meant missing at least two months of prime Stanton season for me.

Before departing, Father turned back to wish us well. He stood in the doorway of our shabby home with his shoulders squared and his spine straight, his round face framed by wavy gray hair and his gray-green eyes full of wisdom and humor. Everything about the scene was familiar, yet something about it tugged at my nerves. He had taken a million trips, what could be different about this one?

Cassie, well rested even after a late night, was the first to step forward. "We'll take care of everything, Father," she promised, her large eyes beaming. Even at twenty-three, she was always eager to please.

"I know you will, my child," he replied, ruffling her golden curls and placing an affectionate kiss on her brow. "And you, my boy," he said, laying a hand on Aaron's shoulder, his expression serious, "you must be the man of the house in my absence."

Any other gangly boy of seventeen might swallow

nervously, his Adam's apple bobbing up and down, but not Aaron. He lifted his chin, puffed out his chest—what there was of it, anyway—and replied, "Of course, Father."

Father took one wary look at me. I could tell he was unsure what counsel to give; we both knew I'd do whatever I wanted. I ignored the apprehension settling in the pit of my stomach and surprised him by going up on tiptoe to kiss him on the cheek. With sugared sweetness, I said, "Be careful, Father, and return as quickly as you can." No one noticed me slip a note into his pocket, a tender missive meant to warm the cockles of his heart and plant in his mind the idea of bringing home something sparkly to go with my new gown.

Smiling absently, he stepped out the door. Aaron and Cassie followed in his wake while I looked on from the doorway, wrapping a shawl more tightly over my nightdress to ward off the goose bumps that erupted on my arms and to stop the prickling of my neck. Father mounted while Aaron held the horse steady. Cassie, doing her best not to cry, reached up to give his hand one last squeeze and smiled lovingly into his face. With a final farewell, he turned the horse toward the woods, put our home and tiny town of Stohl at his back, and rode away.

Camdon lay on the other side of the vast woods. Bleak, dark, and nearly impassable in the cold months, they separated Stanton and the small communities nestled about it on the south from the Dukedom on the north. Skilled travelers could lose their way easily enough in good weather, not to mention winter weather. Luckily, spring had already raised its weary head, so the chance of

Father being caught in a storm was slight. As I watched his horse disappear into the distance, I prayed that he would return to us quickly and safely.

Weighed down with worry, I turned to face our cottage. Even with its trim wooden exterior, small, bright windows, and the spring buds nodding from the flower beds that edged the front door, it seemed less cheerful without Father. It had always been somewhat shabby and outdated, but now, even as the sun climbed higher in the sky, it seemed as if the lights had been extinguished.

The sound of contented animals greeted me as I made my way to the front door. Tucked into snug pens and the small barn beside the house, how could the milk cows, the sow and her piglets, and the hens know that their master had ridden away? Aaron was there to care for them, after all, so it was of little consequence to them. With growing unhappiness, I made my way back to my room, curled up on the bed, and did my best to shut out the rest of the world.

Cassie and Aaron persuaded, cajoled, and finally demanded that I help with the chores while Father was away. One week later, after days of hopelessly damaged dishes, agitated milk cows, chickens let loose on the neighborhood, and our main room peppered with ash and live cinders instead of a well-cleaned hearth, they gave up and decided to take on the extra work themselves. I attended to my regular chores of dusting, straightening worn cushions, and occasionally sweeping the floor, but everything else fell to my siblings.

With everyone busy about me, I had ample time for daydreaming about the stunning gowns, delicate slippers, and brilliant baubles that would lead to my ultimate goal: marriage to a wealthy gentleman. Becoming mistress of a grand mansion with countless servants to do my bidding (and never again setting foot in this cottage) was all I had ever wished for.

It pained me that the balls and social events would carry on without me, but there was nothing to be done about it. Father's decree had been clear enough: we could afford neither the time nor the expense of participating in Stanton's social events until he returned.

Weeks passed in this manner, my days spent in bed or, when I did arise, daydreaming in the window seat or perusing the shops in town for wares I couldn't afford, while Cassie and Aaron took care of the household responsibilities. I didn't dare ask Cassie for an extra penny to buy something pretty, for even I was aware that our supplies were running low. Cassie began to weave again, cutting the price of her cloth to sell it more quickly, and Aaron parted with some of his prized inventions to bring more money. Meanwhile, Father's trip, planned for two months, had already stretched to three, and it had been weeks since we had received word from him.

My knees drawn up to my chest, I perched on the window seat, the glass frigid where it pressed into my spine, and contemplated the problem. Normally, I'd be imagining the life I deserved, filled with handsome gentlemen bowing to my every whim and sophisticated ladies praising my superiority. However, my father's prolonged absence kept pulling my mind from these pleasant pursuits.

A chill seeped into my bones. I twisted around, pressed a hand to the glass, and peered out. Nothing but dreary, impenetrable blackness. The weather had turned unseasonably cold for late spring. A wild wind rattled the glass beneath my palm, hammering the sides of the house with tree limbs and debris. Shivering, I abandoned my place to huddle near the fire with my brother and sister. Engaged in conversation, they barely noted my presence.

"What will we do, Aaron? Father should have returned weeks ago. And now, with this weather . . ." Cassie pulled an old quilt around her shoulders for warmth, her expression grim in the firelight. I knew she wasn't thinking of us, but of Father, stranded outdoors somewhere. Her brow furrowed, but she kept her voice calm. "We're nearly out of food, and I have no more materials to weave fabric with."

"I'm out of supplies as well," Aaron replied, focusing on our present discomforts and skirting the issue of Father's safety like his eldest sister had. For the first time, he looked young, his green eyes fearful. The gravity of their conversation frightened me. How would we survive if Father didn't return soon? What would we do if he never returned?

The answer to our dilemma came to me at once. My collection of fine gowns and shoes—the only things of value left in the house—must be traded for enough provisions to see us through. Survival was more important than a closetful of beautiful things, wasn't it?

I clamped my mouth shut, balking at the idea of sacrificing all I held dear. Why should my prospects be ruined and my dreams left unrealized? Who would love me without my beautiful things? If Father didn't return soon and our circumstances worsened, they'd be my only chance to escape this life.

A knowing voice within me whispered, *Your dreams will be dashed soon enough.*

I brushed it aside, glancing expectantly from Cassie to Aaron and waiting for them to formulate a plan. They were brilliant. Surely they would find a solution. But instead they sat lost in their thoughts, and a choking silence filled the room, creating an eerie stillness against the wind raging outside.

At that moment, the front door burst open and banged thunderously against the wall. A chill raced up my spine, and my whole body tensed. I could hear the shriek of terrified animals sounding from the barn, and I forced myself to face the empty doorway, fighting the paralyzing terror that held me prisoner. My heart nearly leapt out of my chest as a shadowy form staggered over the threshold.

"Father!" Aaron and Cassie cried together. Quicker to recover from their shock than I was, they ran to him. Cassie embraced him, and Aaron forced the door closed before throwing his arms around both of them. I kept my distance, preferring to stay curled up on the firelit hearth, allowing relief to wash over me while my heart resumed beating at its normal pace.

Father looked chilled to the bone. Cassie and Aaron helped him change into dry clothes, settled him into his own bed in the next room, and covered him with layer upon layer of heavy quilts. I crept after them, observing their ministrations from the doorway. Even warm and dry, Father's teeth chattered madly, a sound that left me ill at ease. Cassie pulled hot bricks from the fire where we warmed them each night. Wrapping them carefully, she placed them at his feet. Only then did Father drift into a fitful slumber.

Something was terribly wrong, but none of us could find words to discuss it. Cassie and Aaron kept vigil at Father's side, their movements small and their voices muted. Unable to sleep, I returned to the fire, wrapped myself in the blanket Cassie had set aside, and poked at the embers until the last one winked into darkness.

I awoke with the first rays of dawn. My whole body ached from sleeping on the hearthstone. Stretching resulted in the pops and creaks usually indicative of great age. As quietly as possible, I made my way to Father's bedroom. Everyone was still asleep, Aaron snoring loudly from a chair in the corner and Cassie—still managing to look like an angel—curled up on the floor beside Father's bed. The nerves of the previous day settled in my stomach. They would not allow me to rest until I knew if Father was better. Even in sleep his brow was furrowed and his coloring was slightly gray, so I knew there was nothing to be done. Throwing a heavy shawl over my shoulders, I did what I had refused to do for months and attended to the morning chores.

Only when the animals had been fed, the two cows milked, and a fresh kettle set to boil did anyone else awaken. Cassie, Aaron, and I ate yesterday's bread and sipped tea in silence, our thoughts absorbed by Father's reappearance. Without talking, we rattled around the house, garden, and barn, waiting for something to happen.

Father didn't awaken until much later. The toll the journey had taken was evident in his wan, thin face, the sparse growth of gray beard dotting his chin, and the dullness of his eyes. His frame—previously sturdy and solid from daily labor—had diminished, leaving him bony and gaunt. His gaze skittered over us, his mind far away.

I watched from the doorway as Cassie forced him to drink some broth. A bit of the normal brightness returned to his eyes and his color warmed slightly as he did so.

"My children," he said, his voice scraping like rusty hinges.

"Father!" Cassie cried in relief, throwing her arms around him. "We were so worried about you! What happened?"

He stiffened at the question.

Cassie placed a reassuring hand over his. Her white, delicate fingers contrasted with his brown, work-worn ones like day and night. "Perhaps if you begin at the beginning?" she coaxed. Her gentle touch and calming tone seemed to lend him strength.

With a sigh of resignation, he told us how swift the journey to the Duke of Camdon's estate had been, how his speedy arrival had provided more than ample time to fulfill the duke's wishes. The duke was pleased with his work, and when it was time to depart, he provided

Father with goods and provisions for the return journey. Promising to send for Father when the need arose, he gave him an even larger payment than they had agreed upon and sent him on his way.

"He treated me with the utmost respect," Father mused before lapsing a silence.

Aaron brought him back with an impatient, "What happened next, Father?"

A haunted look crept over Father's face. The shadows beneath his eyes deepened. "All was well. I figured I would arrive home within a fortnight, and since it was warm, I slept outdoors."

Something inside me tensed for the worst. *Here it comes*, the voice inside me muttered.

"One evening, after I stopped for the night, something spooked the horse."

We waited for him to speak. When he didn't, Aaron prompted him with, "What was it?"

"It was too dark," he explained. "I . . . I don't know where the horse went or why." He swallowed. "And when I tried to find him, I got lost."

Lost in the woods? We'd heard countless stories of travelers getting lost in the woods. At best they had to wait until someone passed by. At worst—

"That's when I saw it."

"What did you see?" Cassie asked, her voice resonating with apprehension.

Father focused on her, his eyes dreamy and one corner of his mouth curving up. "It was shining in the undergrowth and it reminded me of your letter, Bella." He tried to locate me in the room, a tiny smile tugging on his lips.

My heart panged with guilt, and I leaned farther into the shadowy recesses of the doorway to escape his sight.

When he couldn't locate me, he continued as if he had. "It was the most stunning jewel." His voice held a wistful quality. "Bright even in the moonlight." He paused again, closing his eyes tightly. "But as soon as I touched it, the forest fell silent."

I held my breath, thinking of all the horrors of the forest.

"I heard a growl. It was a . . . a monster." He opened his eyes, and stared blindly ahead. Motioning with his hands, he said, "It was dressed in rags and covered with hair."

"It was a man, then?" Cassie asked tremulously.

Tears began to roll down Father's cheeks as he relived the nightmare. "I don't know. I only know he was strong." His cheeks damp, his eyes wide, and his chest heaving, he said, "He dragged me back to his mansion and locked me in the dungeon."

My conscience—something I didn't know I possessed—seized at the tale. My father had put himself in danger to appease my wishes and had suffered for it. I could not quiet my tongue; I had to know the rest. "How did you escape?"

He turned to me, surprise widening his eyes when he found me standing alone in the doorway. He released his breath all at once, the words spilling out with it. "He set me free."

None of us spoke, though a palpable air of confusion hung in the room.

Sucking in a long breath, Father plowed on. "I was

mad with hunger and loneliness, hearing strange voices arguing in the night . . ." His voice was low, somewhere between a whisper and a sob. "I'm not sure what I said, but in the end, he let me go."

Cassie, ever the comforting soul, stroked his hand. "It's over," she said. "You need never speak of it again, Father. You are home, and we will care for one another now."

At this, a cry issued from his lips. He buried his face in his hands as fresh tears coursed down his cheeks and muffled his words. "It will never be over."

"What do you mean?" Aaron asked, leaning anxiously over Father's bed.

Father looked up with eyes devoid of hope. "He only let me go on the condition that I return as his servant." His words hung in the air, clear and terrible. "I gave my word."

The horrible truth crashed on me. Father was the most honorable man I knew. If he had given his word, nothing any of us could do or say would change his mind, even if it meant we would never see one another again. Fresh on the heels of this realization was another: I loved my father more than I had ever believed. My heart sank at the thought of never seeing him again.

Cassie threw her arms around him again and buried her face in his chest. "You cannot go, Father! You aren't well!" Her tears mingled with his as they cried, wrapped in one another's arms.

After a moment, Father regained control of his emotions. "It's the only way," he said, stroking Cassie's bright hair. "The jewel I found was his. To pay for taking it, I must serve him the rest of my days."

"You didn't mean to take it. Couldn't you have given it back or paid him off?" Aaron asked.

Father shook his head slowly. "It's not that simple, my boy."

My own face was wet with tears now, their salty tang on my lips. Cassie, nestled against Father's chest, voiced the sentiments of my heart. "It's not fair," she sobbed.

A sad smile lit Father's face. "Life seldom is, my child. I am only grateful that the heavens saw fit to let me see you one last time." He looked us over, his weary eyes shining with pride.

Pulling himself up, he motioned toward the bag he brought with him, which lay unheeded where he had dropped it the day before. "Fetch my satchel, Aaron. Our time together may be short, but we may as well celebrate."

Aaron hesitated for a moment, casting a concerned look at Cassie.

"You need to rest, Father," she said. "Celebrations can wait until you are well."

"Nonsense," Father replied, forced strength in his voice. "I'm not going to die, child." He nodded to Aaron.

The bag Aaron set before him a moment later looked ready to burst. Unfastening the clasp, Father dipped his hands inside, the sorrow in his face lightening. He pulled forth something filmy and delicate and handed it to Cassie.

Her face glimmering with girlish delight, she unfolded it to reveal the most beautiful gown, shimmering and gauzy as fairy wings—so different from the heavy fabrics in fashion.

"It's gorgeous," she said softly, brushing the silvery fabric against her cheek.

"It is to be your wedding dress," Father said, cupping her chin with one palm. "I may not be there that day, but my heart will be with you, my daughter."

Cassie's chin wobbled in an obvious struggle against tears as Father reached into the pack again.

"Now, my son," he addressed Aaron, "for your trade." He pulled forth gleaming tools, fine and new, wrapped in a leather cloth. "And so that you may provide for your sisters in my absence."

Aaron fingered the tools, manfully holding back his emotions. Only a slight tremor in his voice betrayed his feelings. "Of course, Father."

My brother and sister's faces, so recently full of grief and apprehension, shone with fascination as they fingered their beautiful things. My heart thumped in my chest and an idea too beautiful and horrible occurred to me.

"And now, Bella, my child," he said, seeking me out again. "Are you not curious to see what I have brought you?"

Something inside me trembled with excitement—the part that always wanted more, the part that was never satisfied. But something else held me back, a feeling of foreboding souring my stomach. Father motioned me closer, cupping something in his hands. My baser nature drove me forward, eager to catch a glimpse of what lay hidden in his palms. As I came to stand beside him, he let an enormous red pendant swing free, catching the light and making it dance across the walls as it dangled from a golden chain.

"Isn't it lovely?" he asked.

"Is that—" Cassie began before Father hushed her.

The instant I saw the jewel, I was smitten by its beauty. Unable to tear my gaze from it, I slipped it on. My siblings' stares of disapproval grated on my nerves. Ignoring them and pleading weariness, I kissed Father on the cheek, thanked him for the gift, and retired to my room to enjoy my newfound bounty in private.

I passed the afternoon watching rainbows flit across the ceiling and walls as I tipped the jewel this way and that in the sunbeams. The admiration the necklace would garner when I wore it to the next ball would be unmatched. The women's jealousy would be nearly as delicious as the men's glances of approbation.

That night, the jewel drove sleep from my mind, the joys of the afternoon fading with the sun's rays. The stone weighed heavily on my chest like a guilty conscience, pressing the air from my lungs. At sight of the jewel, I had been unable to think of anything else, including the man who had brought it to me. He'd looked so weak when he'd arrived, so different from the hero of my childhood. The question none of us wanted to ask echoed through my mind: Would he die because of what had happened to him?

The door of the bedroom opened and candlelight spilled in from the hallway. Cassie entered and sat heavily on her bed.

"Cass?" Aaron called.

"Yes?"

He leaned in the doorway. "How is he?"

She rubbed her hand over her face. "All right, I think.

His chill is gone and there's no fever. He's sleeping soundly now."

"Thank heavens."

Cassie patted the spot beside her. A second later, the springs creaked beneath his weight.

"And what will we do about . . . ?" Aaron's question hung in the air.

"About?"

I couldn't be sure, but it looked as if he motioned toward me.

"You know she asked him for it," Aaron's husky whisper sounded through the dark room.

"She didn't know this would happen," Cassie replied.

"She probably doesn't even care. You saw the way she behaved today—cold and distant, despite her own father's suffering. He nearly *died*, Cassie." There could be no doubt that they were speaking of me. I blinked back tears at the bitterness in my brother's voice.

"She was very withdrawn . . ." Cassie said uncertainly. "Maybe she feels sorry for what happened."

Aaron snapped back, "How can you defend her after the way she seized that necklace? Though Father wouldn't say, you know it was the same jewel that nearly cost his life."

I squeezed my eyes shut, the truth settling like a rock in my stomach. The afternoon replayed in my mind: the necklace claiming my attention while the man who had sacrificed everything for me lay ill in the other room. Had I even spared a thought for him? As if in condemnation, the stone lay cold against my skin, creating a clammy spot where it pressed against my chest. Could it be the same stone Father had been punished for stealing? Even as I assured myself that it couldn't be the same jewel, an awful foreboding seeped into my mind, whispering that Father would be indebted to a monster for the rest of his life because of me.

"True . . ." The waver in Cassie's voice was audible. I prayed her better nature would win out, even though misgivings twisted my stomach.

"She should pay the price for her actions." Determination rang in Aaron's steely tone.

I wanted to stopper up my ears, blot out the conversation, but it was already too late. There was no way to undo what had already been said or to quiet the emotions roiling within me in confirmation.

With three simple words, my own sister betrayed me.

"Maybe you're right."

Unable to bear another thought, I buried my head under my pillow and allowed the tears to fall freely. With rising panic, questions arose at the back of my mind. Could I allow Father to pay the price for my greed? What would I do if they followed through? How could I escape their condemnation when my heart agreed with them? How could I treasure a jewel that had wreaked such havoc in the lives of my loved ones? My mind reeled from one to another until I fell at last into a troubled sleep.

In the morning, rustling noises drew me awake. I turned to see Cassie rifling through my drawers and stuffing clothing into a rucksack. It wasn't even dawn yet. "What are you doing?" I muttered groggily.

She turned to me, guilt spreading across her face. "I'm so sorry, Bella," she said, "but it's for the best." The discussion from the night before rushed back to me. I dressed quickly and twisted my hair into a bun before stepping into the main room, where Cassie had disappeared to, bag in hand.

Cassie stood beside the front door, shuffling her feet. Aaron stood stern and resolute beside her. "We won't let Father return to that place. You will go instead," he said firmly. I looked to Cassie for help, but she cast her eyes down. I saw her brush a hand over them and heard a muffled sob as Aaron pulled the bag from her grasp. He thrust it at me. "The directions Father gave us are in the pack, and the horse is saddled. You should go before Father awakes."

A million thoughts played through my mind, but my hands closed around the sack automatically. I wanted to argue, to declare that none of this was my fault, but I couldn't force the lie to my lips. Turning away from them, I fumbled for my cloak. Then I let my feet carry me out the front door. It clicked shut behind me, muting my sister's sobs.

I blinked into the sunlight, the shock of what just occurred settling over me. How could I be expected to leave all I knew and turn myself over to a beast? On the other hand, how could Father, especially in his weakened state, be allowed to do so either? My thoughts warred with one another.

I stole a glance behind me at the worn cottage door. Placing a hand on its surface, I fingered the boards, feeling the ridges and pits that had been etched there since my childhood. The wood was as unyielding as the expression my brother had worn; it would not permit me to pass through and return to the life I'd led yesterday. There was no way to go but forward. But perhaps in doing so, I could save my father from his fate.

Three

I felt numb. The jostling of the horse beneath me, the chill morning breezes raising goose bumps on my arms, the sounds of the forest awakening around me—I was only vaguely aware of any of it. The blankness within me swallowed my attention, gnawing at me and erasing thoughts of both present discomfort and bleak future prospects. Like a kite struggling against its tether, I had strained to break free of my humdrum life for as long as I could remember. Now that I had been set free, I felt unmoored, directionless, and abandoned to the wind. The faces of my loved ones haunted me: Cassie, beautiful and disapproving; Aaron, youthful and angry; and worst of all, Father, his kind face drawn and sorrowful.

How could they have done this? The question burned within me, my soul rattled by the actions of my so-called loved ones. Then an even greater question prodded at my mind: How could I escape my fate? Returning home was out of the question, but making a bid for my father's freedom meant taking on the role of the beast's servant in his place. With my wits barely about me, I wondered if I could reason with him. Perhaps if I explained the situation and offered him the jewel . . .

What was the use? Not caring where I was headed, I let the reins slide from my fingers and allowed the horse to wander where he would while I fingered the necklace hanging around my throat. What did it matter where I went? The opportunities afforded by Stanton, the comfortable smallness of my village Stohl, and my home and family were lost to me. Who was left to care if I disappeared into the woods, never to be seen again?

I was only dimly aware of late afternoon beams filtering through leaves and the crisp smell of green, growing plants, so I started when the horse shuddered beneath me. The unexpected movement made me conscious of other things: the horse's taut muscles, the nervous twitching of his ears, and the flaring of his nostrils. A strange stillness filled the air, as if something had hushed all the woodland creatures at once. At that moment, something large and black stepped into my path. The horse screamed and reared, flinging me from his back. My head grazed a tree trunk before I landed heavily on the leaf-strewn ground. The horse was gone, leaving me injured and alone in the forest.

Or rather, not alone.

A feral growl sounded, and I looked up to see the light blocked by a massive figure bending over me. As it reached for me, shock and fear overcame me, and my vision faded to black. The last thing I heard was a gruff voice saying, "What kind of trash has he sent me?"

My head was pounding. That, paired with the rough fabric chafing my cheek and the musky scent of wild animal, brought me to my senses. I was being carried, but by whom or what I could not tell, though the gait felt like a man's. A wave of nausea rose from my stomach at all the jostling. Swallowing, I pushed it back down along with my rising panic. Keeping my body as limp and still as possible, I cracked my eyes open to investigate and caught the first real glimpse of my captor. His thick arms holding me in place over his shoulder were covered in matted, fur-like hair encased in ragged clothing. Remembering what my father had said about claws scrabbling at him, my stomach lurched. I summoned the courage to look up mid-bounce, wary about what I might find. His head was covered with black hair hanging in tangled rats reaching past his shoulders. Nothing of a face could be seen from behind. I squeezed my eyes shut, trying not to imagine the cruel eyes and animalistic features that might be there. How could I bargain with such a creature?

"Look at what he's sent me." His voice was strange, deep, and gravelly, as if unaccustomed to forming words.

"Yes, sir," someone striding behind him replied. The other voice belonged to a man, though I could not see him without craning my neck and drawing attention to myself. "She is young, but who's to say she can't do what's needed?"

I felt the monster's chest move as he blew out an impatient breath. "Young? Look at those hands! They're the hands of a spoiled princess." I fought the urge to curl my fingers into my palms.

"Then what will you do with her?" the monster's companion inquired.

"She's going straight to the cellar," he replied. "The old man might have done some good, but I've no use for spoiled brats. Maybe I should drag *him* back to do the work."

"I'm not sure that's wise," his companion commented politely. "But I'm sure you'll do what's best, sir." The creaking of heavy doors sounded, and the sensation of passing from the brightness of the outdoors down into a dark, musty place gripped me. "Will there be anything else?" the man called from above us.

"No, Jack," the one carrying me called back. "Just leave her to me." The doors banged shut, and I heard a bolt slide into place. I willed myself to hold still, though panic caused my heart to leap into my throat at the thought of being trapped with this personage.

We reached the bottom of the stairway, dusty air enveloping us as we entered some type of basement. Without warning, my captor tossed me roughly onto the dirt floor, pushing a surprised "Oof!" out of me as I landed on my backside. I refused to acknowledge the pain, but it distracted me from the apprehension twisting my nerves.

"Hmph," he said, folding his arms across his broad chest and glaring down at me.

I forced myself to remain in place and look up at him instead of scuttling backward. "What do you want with me?" I asked, trying for boldness but sensing the quaver in my voice. "This?" I lifted the jewel slung around my neck to offer it to him.

"No," he replied scornfully. "I want nothing from a useless child like you."

Fury coursed through my veins, and I lifted my chin. After everything I had endured, his insults enraged me. "Do you think I want to be here?" My words rang though the cellar, slightly hysterical even to my own ears. "I had no choice!"

"Retract your claws," he murmured, moving noiselessly toward a set of steps opposite those that lead outside. The animalistic way he moved, fluid and catlike despite his bulky frame, took me by surprise. At that moment I could not decide if he was more man or beast. Whichever he was, he clearly had no use for me.

"You can't leave me here!" I shouted, but the heavy door was already closing, effectively silencing my rant. Fuming in the dank room, I rubbed my temples and reflected on the injustice of the situation. My life had been practically perfect. *Perhaps not perfect*, I mentally amended, my brother's irate expression and the heartbreak spelled out in my sister's eyes still fresh in my mind. Regardless of recent events, my life had, at the very least, been comfortable.

I pictured our small home on the outskirts of Stohl, unremarkable in its plainness. Cassie, having finished the morning chores, would already be setting the bread to rise in the afternoon sunlight, and Aaron would be busy in his shop. Father would probably still be laid up in bed, recovering from the trials he had endured. My eyes ached with unshed tears as I thought of his deeply wrinkled face, his hair whiter than it had been a few months ago, and his large and able hands lying idle atop the blankets. In his state, he probably hadn't even noticed I was gone. I blinked hastily and took a deep breath to keep the tears at bay. The musty odor of my surroundings filled my lungs, muddying my thoughts like dust motes in a beam of light and reminding me of where I was.

To distract myself from thoughts of home, I took in my surroundings. My misery faded to a dull ache as reality set in. The cellar was little more than a dirt dugout lined with heavy ceiling beams and lit by a single window. One set of steps, carved into the earth itself and set with stones, led to two heavy doors. These, I knew, opened to the outside, and I supposed the door my captor had taken connected to the main building.

Could this be the dungeon my father had described—the place that had diminished him to skeletal proportions? I dismissed the notion, attributing the overexaggerations to my father's illness. Other than being dank and unpleasant, it was nothing like a real dungeon—much more like a storage room where one might place unwanted items, like the broken crates and empty sacks littering the floor.

Like me.

I fingered the necklace at my throat, and my father's face—lined and tired, but dear—filled my mind again. He was the only man who had ever truly loved me. What would happen when he understood what my siblings had done? Would he rejoice at being released from his obligations to my captor? Would he mourn my loss, or would he feel relief at his freedom? Some niggling part of me argued that I had done little to merit the love he'd offered, but I banished that thought, knowing it would only plunge me deeper into despair.

I pulled myself to my feet, shook the dust from my skirts, and forced myself to focus on the problem at hand: how to get out of this wretched place. Making my way to the outside doors first, I heaved against them and heard the telltale rattle of a chain. The doors were both bolted and securely chained in place. My jail was indeed secure.

I tried the other door, which was at the top of a roughly hewn stone staircase. No amount of pushing and pulling could make the portal budge. I glanced up at the sole window in the room, which was pitifully tiny and high up in the wall. Not a single item in the room was tall or sturdy enough to reach it.

Panic flickering at the edge of my mind urged me to find another means of escape, but I knew there was none to be found.

Silly child, the mocking voice at the back of my mind uttered. *Where would you go anyway?*

With a growing sense of hopelessness, I sat down in the center of the room on an itchy burlap sack. I tented my knees before me and wrapped my arms around them. I squeezed my eyes shut and tried to focus on something other than my current predicament or the home that was now too far away to reach. Bending my mind to the task, I conjured up Stanton's ballroom and held it there, examining every detail—elegant draperies, warm candlelight, the rich scent of hors d'oeuvres. I held onto the image as tightly as I could until the memory of the last ball unfolded, filling my mind and senses. Reliving the night, I drifted as gently as a bubble through the vision, my sapphire-blue gown swishing more pleasantly than all my others had.

After a time, my nostrils filled with stale air instead of the tangy richness of delicacies, and my muscles tensed against the reality lurking on the other side of my eyelids. How long I was lost in the memory I couldn't say, only that my eyelids felt scratchy, as if I had been crying and the lashes had become pasted together. Pondering the cause of the tears pulled me back to the present, though I fought to keep my mind far away, safe in a place of beauty and elegance.

"Wake up," A gravelly voice sounded above me, accompanied by the none-too-gentle nudging of a foot to my side. My ribs, already sore from the day's mishaps, protested intensely. I cracked my eyes open to see an impossibly large shadow bending down to place an earthenware bowl before me. *My captor.* My mind skittered away from the thought and focused instead on the bowl.

"What's this?" I muttered.

"Dinner," he said, his tone conveying precisely how stupid he found the question.

I must have wasted the afternoon away with my dreams, for the cellar was shadowy in the evening twilight coming through the window. The only other source of illumination was the lamp my captor had left burning at the top of the steps. I tipped the bowl so I could see inside, sniffed at the watery contents, and poked tentatively at what appeared to be a blob of fat floating on the surface. "I can't eat this," I said disdainfully, releasing the bowl so the gruel sloshed against the sides.

He huffed in response, as if I had just proven his point. "Suit yourself, princess," he growled, turning to leave.

Maybe it wasn't the ideal moment, with him thinking me an idiot—and pampered princess, to boot—but I spoke anyway. "Wait."

He trained his gaze on me, his expression unreadable under the layers of matted hair but the contempt in his eyes was unmistakable.

"You need a servant." The statement shot out, unadorned by elegant persuasive terms. But it was my only chance. He had rejected the only item of value in my possession. All I had left to barter with was my life.

He folded his arms across his chest, regarding me coldly. I dragged my gaze from his razor-sharp nails and swallowed.

"I can clean," I said, the words tumbling out of their own accord. "I can do whatever you need if you'll let me out of this place." My mind had frozen, the desire to leave the cellar so strong that it silenced every other rational thought.

Low, humorless laughter sounded, raising the hair on the back of my neck. "You?" He spat the word out like an insult. "Look at those dainty hands." He jerked his chin toward them. "You've never worked a day in your life."

His words and his awful laughter awakened something inside me, something fiercer than the desperate need to escape: my pride.

"Enough!" I yelled, surging to my feet, hot anger overwhelming the fear I felt in his presence. "First you imprisoned my father, and now you drop me here like a piece of garbage?" I stepped toward him, glaring up into his face, my hands balled into fists at my sides. "You're nothing but a beast!"

Cold laughter issued from the place where his mouth was hidden, sending a chill down my spine. "And you are nothing but a spoiled, angry child. Say what you will; I have no use for you." He turned to leave.

I grabbed his arm, surprised at my own brashness. "No one tells me what I can or cannot do, no matter what they think of me."

His eyes locked with mine, and a flicker of com-prehension—some appreciation for what I was going through—flashed across them. Just as quickly, it dis-appeared, and his face grew stony and implacable once more. He brushed off my hand as one would an insect and turned away again. "As you wish, princess," he said, heading up the stairs. "Tomorrow you may cook and clean to your heart's content." The door swung shut, but not before I heard him mutter, "I will enjoy seeing those pretty hands ruined."

The room fell into darkness once more, and a shiver ran up my spine. I made my way back to the burlap sack I'd been resting on, the anger that had fueled my out-burst draining away and leaving a hollow spot some-where in the region of my heart. *Daddy*, a voice within me whimpered, an echo of the little girl I had once been. I clenched my teeth against it and all the feelings it dredged up, focusing instead on how my family had abandoned me, leaving me with no other recourse but to call on the mercy of a monster.

I tucked my skirts around my legs to deter rodents from nestling into the sack with me. In fairy tales, princesses befriended mice and birds, which then protected and aided their ladies. But the beast was wrong—I was no princess. No matter how desperate and alone I felt, the company of feral animals would always be unwelcome.

Part of me wanted to admit defeat and continue wallowing in self-pity, but my practical nature refused to succumb to those baser urges. There was no immediate escape from my prison—I couldn't change that—but I had, as far as I could tell, convinced the Beast to let me serve as his maid. And at least my father was safe. Perhaps, given enough time, I could devise a stealthier exit and reunite with him. I hugged my knees to my chest and wiled away the night hours imagining the possibilities.

Four

Giddiness practically bubbled out of me as I stepped out of that den of filth. After growling about the dishes, waving me toward the kitchen, and muttering something about ringing the dinner bell when the meal was prepared, my new master deserted me in a drab dining room. I didn't complain. His presence kept my nerves in a state somewhere between horror and intense anger. If I was to play servant, I preferred to do so without him looking on disapprovingly. I surveyed the dirty table and chairs and the grimy window behind them. The skyline afforded by the view looked entirely unfamiliar. Setting aside the idea of escape for the time being, since I hardly knew my location and didn't know which direction to head in to return to Stohl, I determined that it was better to bide my time and play kitchen maid for now. Washing the dishing wasn't exactly a difficult job, I reasoned, stepping toward the kitchen. How many dirty dishes could there be? There were only the two men in the household—my captor and the manservant he'd called Jack the day before.

I was completely unprepared for what I found.

Every surface was piled high with food-caked pots, pans, and utensils. How had they managed breakfast? The notion that using clean dishes wasn't a priority turned my stomach—and made me grateful I had refused the food the night before. My mind conjured up images of gruel slowly creeping out of the bowl of its own accord, and I forced myself to focus on the task at hand. Soon I was too busy to consider anything else.

After a few hours, my hands were reddened and blotchy from the effects of harsh soap, and my muscles complained from carrying load after load of dirty dishes to the sink. I then realized two things: first, I missed that pit of a prison and the forced inactivity it afforded; and second, I had grossly underestimated the ability of two individuals to create a mess.

When I finally scrubbed the last dish and set it to dry with the rest, I was seized by the elation of having accomplished the impossible. Finally uncovering the stove and feeling particularly confident, I began to rummage around for ingredients to transform into an edible meal. I had seen my sister do this countless times over the years. How difficult could it be? My spirits flagged when I saw the poor state of the food in the pantry, and I began to understand why I had only been offered gruel. Vowing to create something more savory, I lit the stove, placed a pot of water on to boil, and dumped in some tough-looking salted meat. Anything would be sufficiently tender, I reasoned, if it was boiled long enough.

While the water was heating, I gathered some battered-looking vegetables, pulled out a newly clean knife, and began chopping. My hands, raw from the dishwater, protested as I hefted the heavy knife. *So much for being a lady,* I thought, noting the sorry state of my palms and swabbing perspiration from my forehead with a sleeve. It would all be worth it if I could produce a decent meal. A short while later, while dishing hot soup into bowls and slicing crusty bread to serve alongside it, I actually felt proud of my efforts.

Judging by the late afternoon light streaming into the kitchen, it was close to or past suppertime. I set the table, served the meal, and pulled the cord connected to the dinner bell. To my dismay, a loud clanging sounded throughout the residence, followed by a heavy thump as the bell abruptly stopped. I glared at the cord. Even if it meant calling everyone to dinner myself, I was never pulling it again.

"Trying to break the bloody bell, are we?"

My new master tromped into the dining room, another man trailing slightly behind. I studied this new man curiously, interested to see the type of person who would choose to live with and serve my captor. He was tall and broad shouldered, with the muscular physique indicative of hard labor. He would have been considered a large man in almost any circle, but compared to his master he looked average. He had dark, rumpled hair, a strong jaw defined by a trim mustache and beard, and intelligent brown eyes. If it weren't for his common attire, he might have passed for a gentleman.

When I ignored his comment on the bell, my captor pointedly ignored me as he entered and seated himself at the head of the table. His silence might have affected me more if his companion hadn't distracted me.

"Hello, Bella. I'm Jack." Apparently he already knew who I was. I remembered the conversation between him and my jailor when I'd been carried from the woods into the cellar.

He treated me to a wide grin. "This looks lovely," he said, motioning to the laden table.

His master grunted his disapproval.

I ignored his ill behavior. "I regret that it has taken so much time to prepare the evening meal." I stared directly at my new master. "The kitchen, dishes, and pantry were in a deplorable state."

Another grunt, louder this time, greeted this remark.

Jack recaptured my attention. "I am sorry about that. It is only the two of us, and we do our best to manage. But it seems you have succeeded in one day what we have failed for years." He grinned again. "Shall we?" Pulling out a chair, he waited for me to sit before taking his place across from me.

The scowl on his master's face only intensified at this maneuver.

I looked on anxiously as the meal began, my own spoon poised halfway to my mouth. I had long ago become adept at reading body language, and even the layers of hair and beard couldn't hide the disapproval in my captor's demeanor as he sniffed the soup. He took one spoonful, spat it back into the bowl, and pushed it scornfully aside.

"Are you trying to poison me?" he declared with a glower. "What did you put in this?"

Out of the corner of my eye, I saw Jack cast him a glance.

"Are you trying to tell me this is edible, Jack?" he snapped, settling the weight of his glare on his manservant.

Setting my own spoon down with a thump, I folded my arms across my chest, narrowed my eyes at my host, and pronounced, "You really are a beast."

He laughed, a low, sardonic sound that made the hair on the back of my neck prickle. Propping his booted feet on the table, he leaned back in his chair. "Of course, princess. That's all you can see, isn't it?"

Is there anything else to see? I wanted to demand, but the dangerous gleam in his eyes warned me to keep quiet. Instead, I turned my glare on the filthy boots muddying the table I'd worked so hard to clean. I considered shoving them off. Hard.

"You are entitled to your opinion," he said, drawing my attention. "You may even call me a beast if you desire, as long as you continue to clean my home. It seems you are not entirely inept in that area, though I am pleased to see that Your Highness has already spoiled her delicate hands." He chortled as he gazed at my splotchy palms. I couldn't help pushing them under the table and looking away.

I had never encountered someone so contrary. I was relieved when he turned away from me to discuss something about the property with Jack. With his keen eye directed elsewhere, I started in on my own bowl of soup.

It looks all right, I thought, noting the colorful vegetables floating on top, interspersed with bits of meat. But with the first spoonful, I understood why the Beast had spit it out. The flavor was somewhere between yesterday's wash water and the contents of the slop bucket. Refusing to give him the satisfaction of admitting how awful it was, I choked down every drop and ignored my stomach's protests.

Jack, for his part, dutifully dug into a generous portion of the unpalatable soup and tooth-shatteringly hard bread. He shoveled spoonful after spoonful into his mouth as though it was the best thing he had ever eaten. That act alone endeared him to me.

Having completed his conversation, the Beast departed without another look at me, tromping out as noisily as he had come in. I was left once more with a pile of dirty dishes.

"Let me help you with those," Jack offered, reaching to take the plates from my hands. Between the Beast's imposing physique and abrasive personality, and the utter failure of a meal that I had just served, I had not expected such kindness.

"That's not necessary," I said, feeling guilty. It was my fault he'd had to eat that terrible meal.

"I insist," he said, carrying the dishes to the sink. "I'm sure you've had a tiring day."

My good breeding dictated that I turn the conversation back to him, so I commented politely about how his day had likely been challenging as well, but as I followed him to the kitchen, I caught a reflection of myself in the window glass, and all ideas of politeness were driven from my mind. Bits of hair had sprung free of my bun and stuck haphazardly to my face and neck. My eyes were smudged with dark shadows, and my nose was burnished red from the heat and exertions of the day. *Attractive*, I thought bitterly, remembering how my sister's hair curled alluringly at the nape of her neck, her cheeks flushed a becoming pink, and her eyes glowed bright blue when she grew overheated. I gazed at the limp brown hair and hazel eyes of my reflection. I was a copy of my father in female form, complete with his tendency to sweat profusely. I sighed, thinking longingly of the glittering jewels and rich fabrics that lent distinction and refinement to my features. Without them, I was ordinary.

Absentmindedly, I fingered the large red jewel hanging around my neck. The Beast hadn't wanted it for whatever reason, and I was grateful. It was the only thing of beauty left to me, though its vibrancy clashed with the faded figure reflected in the window.

"Anything else I can do?" Jack asked, after washing the dinner dishes and laying them out to dry.

"No," I said quietly, pulling my gaze from the homely girl in the glass to meet his eyes.

"He's not as terrible as he seems," Jack commented after a moment, probably assuming that his master was the source of my dark contemplations. "All of us are somewhat beastly, you know," he added.

"He just wears his beastliness where everyone can see it."

To my surprise, he chuckled, his eyes crinkling at the corners. "At least you know what you're getting into, right?"

I wish, I thought. To be honest, I was entirely out of my element. I felt as if everything was spinning danger-ously out of control and I could do nothing to stop it. Not that I would admit it to a man who was practically a stranger.

"If it's any consolation, you're doing wonderfully," he reassured me.

I couldn't help it; I laughed out loud. "You're right," I said, sarcasm flavoring my tone. "Wasn't that meal delectable?"

He chuckled again. "I have every confidence in your abilities," he said as he made his way out the door.

I chewed my lip as he closed the door behind him. Compared to the other compliments I'd received over the years, this didn't even rank in the top twenty. But for some reason, Jack's simple words brought a smile to my face. Maybe there really was something genteel about him.

Although the dishes were all clean, the task of stor-ing them now lay before me. I knew I'd have to wipe years of grime off the shelves and cupboards that lined the kitchen walls before I could even start putting things away. Perhaps it was my haunted face in the window or the fact that the work was more challenging than I had imagined, but the job dragged on, my hands more slug-gish than before. In an effort to divert myself, I brought my father's face to mind as it had once been: round and full, his cheeks creased with smile lines, and his gray-green eyes bold. I pictured him in the doorway of our home, ready to embark on the trip that had turned everything upside down.

The image of Cassie and Aaron as they watched Father depart contrasted greatly with their demeanor at my departure. Thinking of the two events filled my heart with bitterness. *How could they have done this?* I slammed the cutlery drawer with far more force than necessary.

As if on cue, the Beast appeared, disapproval painting his features. I was again struck by the uncanny way he popped out of nowhere—the same way a wolf noiselessly tracks its prey. *Am I the prey?* I thought uneasily as he glared down at me, his eyes boring a hole in my chest. I prayed he was only looking at the large jewel that hung about my neck.

"May I help you?" I asked, unable to endure his silent leering a moment longer.

His eyes snapped up to mine, almost as if he'd forgotten I was there. "It's nighttime."

I glanced out the window, noting the darkened sky. Hours had passed since dinnertime. "So it is," I said. His presence filled me with a mixture of fear and irritation that I was beginning to expect. Concealing it the best I could, I responded, "I suppose you're here to escort me back to the dungeon?"

Grim humor glimmered in his eyes. "If that's what you want, princess," he said, crossing his arms over his broad chest. "Though Jack informs me it is hardly fitting. This afternoon he located your horse and retrieved your things. He's readied a room for you, but if you'd prefer the cellar . . ."

"*No!*" I winced as the word shot out, embarrassed that

I couldn't hide my reluctance to return to that dank pit, even after hours in a dirty kitchen. "That's most . . . accommodating of you," I managed, recovering some courtesy at last.

"It's not my doing," he said gruffly, turning away.

"All the same, I thank you."

He *hmphed* and mumbled something about seeing me to my room before striding off.

I followed him upstairs to an ancient bedchamber with a creaky door and dilapidated furnishings, the most prominent of which was a sagging bed draped with dingy bedclothes. Having recently become an expert on the subject, I recognized the overall color palate of the room as dirty dishwater gray. *How cheerful and welcoming,* I thought. The only items that lent any brightness to the chamber were the garments my sister had stuffed into my pack, which were now hanging neatly in the closet, and various personal items, including a hairbrush and other necessities, which were laid out atop a worn-looking dresser. A lump formed in my throat, whether from the thought of my sister having packed them or Jack having done his best to make the place livable, I wasn't sure. I swallowed, desperate to hold back my emotions.

"A bedroom fit for a queen, wouldn't you say?" the Beast mocked.

"It's perfect," I replied, determined not be bothered by his surliness. If I could win him over, I might be able to convince him to let me return to my family. If the situation became unbearable I could run away, relying on my wits to guide me home.

As if sensing my thoughts, he said, "It's better than

being outdoors. My property is edged by forest, and the nearest neighbor is miles away. Only a fool would consider running off alone."

"Who would want to run away when they are treated with such hospitality?" Given a different intonation, the words would have been a genuine compliment to one's host, but my patience was growing thin. From the glint in his eyes, I could tell the Beast understood all too well what I meant.

"Precisely, my lady. It is well you realize how fortunate you are to be afforded such protection and generosity in exchange for your services. Heaven only knows what might befall a poor, defenseless child like you out there."

The words, uttered in a low tone, whipped across me like a threat. I glared up at him, willing my newfound anger to banish the fear within me.

"Even the most humble of God's creatures possesses natural defenses against its enemies," I retorted.

We were now only a few inches apart, nearly nose to nose. Our breaths came out in angry puffs. Our arms crossed over chests.

"I trust everything is satisfactory?"

I jumped, startled to see Jack, who'd materialized almost out of thin air to step into the space between us.

Taken aback by his sudden appearance, it took a moment to calm myself enough to respond politely. Inhaling, I avoided the Beast's glare—which would only infuriate me further—and focused on Jack's anxious brown eyes. "Yes," I replied at last. "Thank you for recovering my things."

"It was nothing," he said, smiling—though this time

the expression seemed tight and artificial, his eyes cold and flat behind it. "Is there anything else you'll need tonight?" He was already shooing the Beast from the room, though I heard a low growl of protest as he did so. Jack turned to glance back at me, his hand on the door and the fake smile plastered on his face, waiting for my reply. "No? Then we'll be going. Good night, Bella," he said, hastily shutting the door behind him.

Without thinking, I rushed across the room to press an ear to the wood. The Beast's voice echoed down the hallway. "But I don't like her! She's impossible!"

I heard a hushed reply from Jack, too low to hear. "I don't care!" the Beast snarled back. "She may as well know what I think of her . . ."

As though he had left me any doubt, I thought. Overhearing a conversation about myself—especially one where I was cast in such a negative light—disconcerted me. It brought to mind the midnight interchange between my brother and sister the night after my father returned from his trip. My insides twined painfully at the recollection, and I pushed it to the back of my mind. I prided myself on being immune to others' disapproval, but doing what I wanted without regard for others had now severely damaged my prospects. With the exhaustion of the day weighing on me, I made my way to the bed, threw back the covers, and collapsed onto it. I buried my head under the blankets, seeking to block out the discussion in the hallway and the memories it unearthed.

Five

*M*y fingers, buried knuckle-deep in rich soil, cleared a place for new plants. Pride welled up inside me as I cultivated a miniature paradise in an untidy world. A large hand brushed mine, and I smiled automatically at the light eyes set in a handsome face. An answering smile crept over his lips, as slow and dazzling as a sunrise edging across the sky. He passed me a small rose bush.

"Is this where you'd like the red rose?" I asked, indicating the center of the garden plot.

"Isn't it your favorite?" His voice was deep but soft as a caress. "It should have the place of honor."

"But what of your favorite rose?" I asked coyly. "Where shall we put it?"

His eyes darkened a shade as he leaned forward and wrapped his strong arms around me, the small rose bush dropping unheeded to the ground. "Here," he said somewhat huskily, tucking me under his chin. "I will keep my favorite Rose here."

I awoke, feeling the ghost of warm arms wrapped around me until the predawn chill drove the sensation away. I took a deep breath, willing the last vestiges of the dream to linger. After a moment, only one word remained.

Rose.

In a way I could no sooner understand than define, the name was connected to me. Contrary to the tenor of the dream—safe, secure, beloved—the name carried with it the compulsion to run, to escape this place and the prison it represented. Like a child trapped in the aftermath of a nightmare, I frantically scrambled for the shoes I had kicked off in my sleep and fumbled in the dim light for my wrap. Finally dressed, I calmed my thumping heart enough to listen for the sound of others who might be awake. All was silent. I eased my door open and made my way down the shadowy corridor to the kitchen, flinching with each creak and moan of the old floorboards. The kitchen door led outside, and I exhaled in relief as I cracked it open and felt the coolness of the brisk morning air.

Why didn't I do this before? I asked myself, hurrying across the grounds as one possessed. Yesterday I'd been standing feet from freedom but hadn't felt the urgency to leave. I had been focused on proving myself to the Beast and convincing him to grant me freedom. Now repulsion for him consumed me, along with an the need to put as much space between us as possible. Careless of the noise I made now that I was far from the house, I threw open the stable door. My goal had been to reach the stable, find my father's horse, and leave this place far behind me.

"What do you think you're doing?"

The words made me freeze. My hand halted mid-reach toward the saddle and tack. I turned to face the intruder.

"Jack?" I squeaked. My hand dropped to my chest in relief as I blew out the breath I hadn't realized I'd been holding. Unthinkingly, I stroked the stone at my neck. *Father, soon I'll be with you,* I thought.

"Thank heavens it's you." I smiled up at Jack. "Help me saddle this horse, will you?"

Even in the early morning light, I could tell he didn't return the smile. Instead, his arms were crossed over his chest, and the corners of his full lips were drawn down. The disapproving stance reminded me of someone else—someone who would certainly impede my departure.

"Won't you help me?" My voice betrayed my vulnerability. When my question met no response, I lifted my chin, reached for the saddle, and injected my words with coldness to show how little his betrayal meant. "Then I'll do it myself."

Jack's hand met mine on the bridle, and I looked up into his face, surprised. "I won't let you do this," he said simply. "For your sake as much as his."

Something inside me collapsed at his words, my delicate hope shattering into fragments. Angry tears of disappointment splashed over my cheeks as I realized how alone I was. "Why should he care? I'm nothing more than a servant!" I shouted, all semblance of composure vanishing. I pounded my fists against his chest like a young child throwing a tantrum.

He trapped my wrists in his large hands and gazed into my face, his eyes grave. "He needs you. Don't you understand, Bella? He's lost everything."

"That has nothing to do with me!" I retorted, wrenching my hands free and glaring at him. With as much quiet fury as I could muster, I said, "All I can see is that you won't help me and you won't allow me to leave. You're as hateful as he is." I watched the words sink in, feeling a certain amount of satisfaction as a twinge of pain crossed his face. Spinning on my heel, I strode away from the stable before he could witness the tears washing my cheeks. My dreams of escape crumbling with each step, I made my way back to my bedchamber.

Despite the scratchy bedclothes chafing every inch of my exposed skin, I swore never to leave this bed again. It had witnessed grief at my frustrated escape and anger at Jack's betrayal, and now it cocooned me against the reality lurking outside the door. How long I would be allowed to stay abed before I was summoned to fulfill by responsibilities I didn't know. Only one thing was sure— this was the only place I felt safe.

I was foolish to assume that Jack would serve as my ally against his master. I should have realized the depth of the loyalty he must have to stay in this place. The fact that none of that loyalty extended to me gnawed at my heart. Part of me wondered why he would choose this lonely existence. Another part condemned him as an idiot for remaining at the Beast's side. I lay under the musty covers, smoldering with rage and humiliation as I considered his role in the events of the night before.

Bang! Bang! *BANG!*

I sat up in alarm, the covers clutched to my chest and my eyes fixed on the door. It hung open, still jittering on its hinges from its collision with the wall. I expected an enormous animal to come lumbering through the doorway with mad, wild eyes. In truth, the Beast looked rather sheepish as he stepped over the threshold.

"I'm sorry, I . . ." he faltered, his embarrassment evident.

Had my jaw not already been on the floor, it certainly would have been following this out-of-character apology. I stared open-mouthed, wondering what would happen next. For once, my curiosity was stronger than my fear.

The Beast spread his meaty palms before him in a gesture of submission. "I didn't mean to force the door." His voice was devoid of its customary gruffness. Softer. Like the wolf's melodic howl instead of its threatening snarl. "I understand you had quite a night."

That's an understatement, I thought. I didn't trust this sudden compassion. Steeling myself, I pursed my lips and turned my face to the wall.

"Yes . . ." His voice was low, almost a purr. "That's the sulky child I know."

I whipped around to face him, my body tensing with the ire that had been festering within me since our first meeting. "And how do you know anything about me?" I demanded, a fraction louder than I intended.

"Oh, I've known my share of pampered maids." He

crossed his arms over his chest in his habitually arrogant pose. *Like the mighty bear bullying smaller woodland creatures*, I thought.

Aloud, I said, "Who's to say I'm like the women you knew?"

"Aren't you?" he challenged, taking a step toward me. I flinched back, and some emotion flickered in his eyes. Disappointment, perhaps? Whatever it was, he sailed on as if nothing had happened. "You're the type that assumes your charms are sufficient to ensure that everything in life will be handed to you. You're the type that is happy to watch others slave and sacrifice without offering anything in return." In one quick motion, he stepped up to the bed and swept the jewel from my throat, deftly snapping the chain. He held it aloft, his eyes full of hatred. The red stone glinted in the early afternoon light. "You're the type that covets *things* and devalues people."

I stared up at him, barely remembering to close my mouth. In a matter of seconds, he had succinctly summed up my life's philosophy. Was I really so transparent? How else could he have guessed so accurately?

When I made no contradiction, his eyes—which still held mine—softened, then closed while he drew in a breath and released it. When they again opened, his eyes were calm. "One can always change."

The spell that held me bound burst. "Am I to take advice on bettering myself from *you*?"

Ignoring my jab, he continued patiently, "Have you no pride? No loyalty?" He dropped the jewel on the bed and glared at it. "Perhaps I am not the one to instruct you on bettering yourself, but as one who's met your father, I am certain he provided you with a thorough education."

I could feel my resolve crumbling at the mention of my father. Tears burned my eyes. *Father.* He had reached out to me with perfect love, never asking anything in return. And how had I repaid him? My fingers twitched toward the place where the jewel rested, the tangible reminder of his greatest sacrifice.

"Do you know why he was willing to surrender everything to be my servant?"

I sniffed, unable to meet the Beast's gaze, much less form a reply.

"Because of this." He picked up the stone from the coverlet and thrust it into my face.

"Why?" The word escaped on a breath, even though I was fairly sure I knew the answer.

His voice was soft, almost wistful. "He traded his freedom for this jewel, so that he could give it to you." He let the words hang in the air, reaffirming what I had already guessed. Shaking his head, he added, "How could a man of such honor have a daughter like you?"

I met his gaze again, expecting to find disdain there, but the eyes, which I was surprised to find the soft gray of cloud-shrouded sky, held gentleness. No retort sprang to my lips. The truth was irrefutable.

"Have you no pride, Bella?" he asked again, his voice lighter than before, casting a different meaning on the words. This time it was less of an accusation than it was a challenge to rise above myself and to become something better. Serving well in my father's place, I could become someone of whom even the Beast would approve. It was something I had never aspired to previously.

The question hung between us. The Beast looked intently into my eyes. It lasted only a moment or two, but it felt like eternity. I looked away, lost in my own thoughts. Then I heard the door close quietly. His words echoed in my ears, haunting me. Pulling the necklace from where he had dropped it in my lap, I examined the stone, running my fingers over its smooth surface. The clasp was bent, but that could be easily mended. As I fiddled to repair the chain, I considered my situation.

Did I have the strength to serve as my father would have, faithfully and well? With no immediate means of escape and no clear idea of where I could even go, what did I have to lose in attempting to fill my father's place in this household? Feeling more and more determined, I arose. I scrubbed the tears from my face, slung the jewel around my neck, tied on my apron, and went to work.

Six

The Beast's home was two steps above a run-down hovel—in my estimation, anyway. Dust, dirt, and spider webs clung to every surface. I tried not to dwell on the webs or the scurrying, many-eyed creatures that had left them behind. Instead, garbed in my oldest dress and with my hair tied up in a worn cloth, I worked to eradicate the webs and grime from the premises. It wasn't easy. After leaving one corner of the house spotless, I would return to find the dust and dirt piled up again. In imagination, I saw legions of filthy men tromping through with mud-caked boots, creating the messes I encountered each day. I began to look askance at the Beast and Jack, thinking up dire accusations. Though I wouldn't allow myself to voice them, I comforted myself by allowing them to run through my mind.

I had watched my sister painstakingly care for our household day after day, the task often lasting from sunup to sundown, but I had never realized all the work that went into it. The laundry alone nearly did me in. Like the dirt and spider webs, it seemed to mound up higher and higher until it could no longer be ignored. My hands became chapped from scrubbing the never-ending supply of clothes, bed linens, rags, and other household items. I particularly hated handling the men's clothing; it was so thick with filth and sweat that it could practically walk about on its own. However, after the first few loads of laundry, even this was something I grew used to.

Every day I followed a similar schedule. I awoke early each morning, stepped into my work clothes, and dusted, scrubbed, and washed until midday. Then I'd prepare a simple meal, call the others to eat—though not with the dreaded bell—and clear the table when they finished. I took my own meals in the kitchen, preferring solitude to the company of the glowering Beast or penitent Jack. I did everything in my power to actively avoid the Beast's loyal servant, wounded more than I cared to admit at his refusal to help me. Our barely budding flower of friendship had been crushed under Jack's boot, and as punishment, I refused to speak with him alone. As most of his labors took him outdoors while mine kept me indoors, this wasn't particularly hard to accomplish.

The Beast, on the other hand, was surprisingly difficult to avoid. He took every occasion to comment on a spot of dust I had missed or to unceremoniously eject me from his favorite household haunts. I found his frequent interruptions rather annoying until I began to understand how to get around him. Returning his brusque and often condescending behavior in kind had little effect, so I often had to swallow my pride and do as he bid me. Still, to vent my frustration, I feigned a subservient manner, calling him "master" and assuring him that his every wish was my command. If a certain mocking note lingered in my voice, it really couldn't be helped. It wouldn't put either my position as his servant or my resolve to serve well in jeopardy.

"That lamp needs cleaning," he grumbled one day.

I stared at his long, jagged fingernail pointing at the glass shade and thought that the lamp wasn't the only thing that needed attention. Automatically I replied, "Of course, master. As you wish."

Perhaps I didn't inject the right amount of abject servility into my response. His eyes narrowed. "If you find the work too challenging . . . ," he trailed off, one hand gesturing lazily toward the cellar. *He wouldn't dream of it!* I thought. Was Jack to make his dinner? As mediocre as my culinary abilities were, they were far superior to Jack's. As it was, Jack—who had to be at his duties earlier than I did—was charged with making the morning meal, and the lumpy mass of whatever passed for porridge never failed to horrify me.

Squaring my shoulders and lifting my chin, I met the Beast's gaze. "I am perfectly capable of doing whatever is required, sir." I caught a gleam of amusement in his gray eyes, so fleeting that it might have been a trick of the light.

"Then stop this ridiculousness and get to work." The message might have come across as more absolute had he been able to maintain his usual gruff tone, but his voice was strangely light—almost as if he were trying to stifle laughter. Which was ludicrous, of course. The idea of the Beast possessing a sense of humor was about as improbable as a cat learning to bark and fetch sticks. Whatever the cause of the change in his tone, I pretended not to notice. Good help never does.

"Of course, sir. Right away, sir. Anything else I can do for you, sir?" The words rattled out quickly. I watched him anxiously, afraid I had overstepped the limits of his good humor, but he merely made a disgusted sound deep in his throat and turned away, leaving me to my own devices for the rest of the day.

Afternoons followed the same pattern as mornings: cleaning, scrubbing, and beating dirt out of worn rugs and tapestries until suppertime drew near. Then I would prepare the evening meal. After dinner, any chores that couldn't wait until morning had to be completed before I could stop for the night, make my way to my room, and fall into bed exhausted.

A few things made those first few weeks bearable. First, after that horrible first day, someone kept the pantry stocked with fresh vegetables, meats, and other edibles, which made my amateur attempts at cooking more successful than before. It gave me a certain amount of pride to see everyone tuck in to their meals each day, although the Beast did his best to hide his approval. Jack, on the other hand, was nothing but complimentary of my culinary efforts. But anything was better than his gummy porridge and fatty gruel.

Second, two or three times a week I would find a

steaming bath waiting for me in my room at the end of the day. I had never known how luxurious it felt to soak aching limbs in a hot bath, but it was a pleasure I fully appreciated. I could hardly imagine the Beast running to the market or drawing me a bath, so that left only Jack. His unspoken determination to make my stay as comfortable as possible softened my attitude toward him, and a measure of the warmth I had felt for him at first returned.

My last relief were afternoon daydreams, which helped preserve my sanity. As was my custom at home, I allowed my mind to roam freely while my hands were occupied with menial tasks. Instead of conjuring up wealthy noblemen and beautiful country manors, I enumerated each of the kindnesses showered on me by my family and committed their beloved faces to memory. Falling into my new role had changed my perception of them and all they had done for me. My siblings' offenses—which had once seemed unforgiveable—grew dimmer and less important in contrast. They may have been the reason I no longer had a home to call my own, but I missed them more than I could ever have imagined. Spending my afternoons thinking of them and my father made me feel less alone.

In sleep, however, my mind drifted elsewhere, bringing other faces to the forefront.

I gazed into the glass, twisting one last curl into place on my brow. There, I thought, particularly satisfied. Won't he be pleased? Glossy dark curls ringed my face and spilled down my back, and my warm brown eyes glowed tonight. Dimples blossomed in my cheeks. Barely able to contain myself, I stood to examine my gold gown and to ensure that everything was in place. The tight bodice hugged my figure perfectly, and the elbow-length sleeves edged with ivory lace emphasized the creaminess of my skin.

I preferred the elegance of a train, but there was to be dancing tonight, and managing a train would be bothersome. I inspected the full skirts in the mirror to make sure my petticoats were respectably tucked beneath them and that the dainty satin slippers just peeped out. Giddy with anticipation, I added one last touch: my trademark golden locket engraved with a simple rose, which slipped into place in the hollow of my throat.

Yes, *I thought as I rushed from the room,* he will be very pleased indeed.

I awoke from these dreams with a start, forgetting who and where I was until reality clicked into place. The girl in my dreams had the same graceful hands I'd seen flecked with soil before. She was somehow familiar and unknown at the same time. *Rose.* Her name drifted back to me. She was becoming a tangible comfort to me with her shining eyes, her heart brimming with happiness, and her life the fulfillment of everything I'd ever dreamed.

I contrasted my own experiences with hers. I knew far too well the overwhelming exhilaration of readying oneself for a magnificent event, floating on a cloud of hope through the stately doors and into the elegantly decorated ballroom, praying that *this* might be the night—only to have my hopes dashed within minutes. The last ball I'd attended stood as a grim testimonial.

But Rose—who was as beautiful as Cassie, in her

own way—had probably never known such rude behavior from the gentlemen of her acquaintance as I had. The recollection of my last ball seemed pale and lusterless beside her experiences.

Night after night, I longed to leave my world of never-ending work and escape into her reality. Day after day, however, I bent myself to the tasks before me. Underneath years of grime, I was pleased to discover, was a lovely country home. It would never be as fashionable as the mansions and palaces of my daydreams, but it was sturdy and elegant in its own right. The exterior walls were constructed entirely of carefully cut and fitted gray-blue stone with glass windows glinting in the sunlight. The interior boasted carved mahogany moldings, ancient tapestries, and a variety of charming (if dated) furniture. At some point it had been respectable, but after years of neglect, it had become little more than a shadow of what it had once been. As its beauty began to reemerge, I vowed to do everything in my power to restore it to its former elegance.

I realized early on that the transformation from disorder to decency could only be brought about if the house's inhabitants took part in the process. My daily interactions with the Beast had taught me not to fear his rough manner, and I began to take advantage of his frequent appearances to goad him into doing things that would better the living situation.

While the Beast was stalking the halls one afternoon, I let out a dramatic sigh. The Beast paused warily. He hated my sighs worse than anything, so I saved them for special occasions like this. "What is it, Bella?" he asked flatly.

"Oh, it's nothing. Hardly worth mentioning. I'll get back to work, sir." I turned back to dusting a nearby portrait of a decorated general atop a white stallion.

"Bella . . ." There was a hint of warning in his voice. It was the tone governesses used on unruly wards.

"Well . . ." I said slowly. "If you insist, sir, it's the roof tiles."

"Roof tiles?" he repeated blankly.

"Yes, sir." I wondered how many times I could use the word *sir* in one conversation. My record was fifteen, but I might as well try for twenty. "Several tiles seem to be missing, sir, and the ceiling in the drawing room is leaking."

He groaned and covered his eyes with one hand. The gesture was startlingly vulnerable. My eyes were drawn to the long, dirty clawlike nails curving over his face. I tried to keep from shuddering at the sight of them.

"I'll look into it," he said, so low it was barely audible. He turned to leave, obviously annoyed that I had given *him* something to do for a change.

I couldn't help myself. "And, sir!" I called after him, gratified to see him turn back with impatience plain in his eyes. "Have a lovely afternoon!" Uncomplimentary mutterings drifted back toward me as he slouched away. Unfazed, I relished the momentary victory. Jack soon set about repairing the roof.

It took several weeks of battling the mess and setting the Beast to attend to repairs before I could turn my attention to exploring my new home. Being a girl of inborn curiosity, it was only a matter of time before I nosed my way into every nook and cranny. I was disappointed to find that of the fifteen bedrooms one was much like another, and only three piqued my interest in the least. But exploring them provided another distraction from the monotony of my chores.

The first was Jack's room. His belongings hung neatly in the closet or were stored in a scarred dresser. With the barest twinge of conscience, I rummaged through everything. I knew little of Jack beyond the work he did and his unswerving devotion to the Beast, but surely something in his possession would shed light on who he was and how he'd come to live here. My efforts turned up little beyond the everyday work clothes and boots one might expect. Personal papers, letters from family and friends, and books with intriguing inscriptions were nowhere to be found.

In fact, only one item caught my attention: a small portrait in a battered frame shoved to the back of the bottommost drawer. When I pulled it out, the faces of two young children peered up at me. Done in faint watercolors, it displayed a young Jack—recognizable by his boyish grin and the dark, half-curling locks falling into his eyes—with his arm slung about another boy. Looking at Jack's youthful face, affection welled up inside me. No matter how I tried to smother it, a smile spread over my face. His companion, also dark-haired, but slightly taller and more sturdily built than Jack, was unfamiliar. I stared at the portrait for a long time, noting the wistful expression on the second child's oval face, which contrasted so strongly with the jovial one sported by Jack. The boys were too dissimilar to be siblings, but something in the comradely way they leaned toward one another suggested a close bond. Nothing more about Jack could be gleaned from his sparse bedchamber, but the image of the two boys floated back to me at odd times when I was busy with work. I pictured them playing, getting into trouble together, and slowly growing into manhood. What had happened along the way to force young Jack, a boy with hope and joy shining in his eyes, into a life of servitude?

The next bedroom I determined to explore had a locked door, but the scent of the Beast, a mix of wild animal and pine, hung about it. It had to belong to him. I crouched down to peer through the keyhole but caught little more than a glimpse of worn furnishings: a large, shabby bed, sagging shelves, and countless books scattered about. The books intrigued me. I didn't know the Beast could read, much less entertained any interest in the written word. Focused entirely on the keyhole and trying to learn as much as I could from its narrow view, I was taken by surprise when someone behind me cleared his throat.

I froze.

This is it, I thought. *This is the moment when the crazed monster snaps.* As I stood and turned to face the Beast, my mind conjured up scenarios of what he might do to me. I remembered how effortlessly he had tossed me to the ground when we'd first met, and I tried not to shudder as I turned to meet his eyes. Relief washed over me as I came face-to-face with Jack instead. His eyebrows were knit together, and his mouth formed a grim line.

We were barely on speaking terms, but his presence on this occasion was preferable to his master's.

"I wouldn't do that if I were you," he said simply. "He values his privacy."

My momentary relief was replaced with irritation. "I was just buffing the doorknob," I answered loftily, running my forefinger over the tarnished brass, then rubbing it against my thumb to display the dirt clinging to it. "The way dust collects in this place is scandalous."

"Hmmm," was all he said, narrowing his eyes and looking at me calculatingly. "He will not take kindly to intrusions into his room, Bella."

I pretended not to understand what he meant and replied, "Then he should keep his things a little more tidy." *Like you do*, I nearly added, but I caught myself in time. I had no qualms about snooping through his things, but it seemed unwise to let him know that I had done so.

"Some of us are more like open books than others," he said, looking at me knowingly. He turned to head back down the hall, and I hazarded another glance through the keyhole.

"Bella." His tone was stern, and his dark eyes drilled into me when I looked back at him.

Chastised, I stepped away from the door, tucking my hands behind my back and feeling like a child who had been warned away from a fire, only to be caught inching closer to the flames. Embarrassed, I kept my distance from the door as Jack walked away.

I counted myself lucky. Though the interchange with Jack had not been pleasant, if the Beast had caught me peeping at his things, it would have been much more disagreeable. The locked door still intrigued me, but I heeded Jack's words to avoid it.

I happened upon the last room—the most fascinating of all—almost by accident. Since Jack had only warned me away from the Beast's room, I deemed that everything else was fair game. I had been over the house from attic to cellar many times, and I thought I had entered every room—other than the Beast's bedchamber, of course. When asked, I explained that I was inspecting the wall hangings and floor coverings for needed repairs. This excuse allowed me to wander where I would, and I eventually discovered a door tucked away and forgotten behind a tattered, faded tapestry. The door itself was unremarkable. Cracked paint and a thick layer of dust clung to its surface, testifying of its long disuse. I studied it for a moment, wondering what could be hidden in the remotest corner of the house, far from both the Beast's and Jack's quarters. Glancing down the corridor, I twisted the knob and immediately met resistance. Like the Beast's room, it was locked.

Disheartened, I frowned at the knob. To find something so tantalizing as a secret door and then to find it locked was more than frustrating. *One more time can't hurt*, I thought, and I tried the knob again, pressing my weight against the door for good measure. All at once it gave way with a loud creak, and I tumbled through the doorway, falling face-first onto the floor. Dust billowed into the air, covering me and inducing a coughing fit. Rubbing my eyes and taking shallow breaths, I recovered enough to look around. At first glance, it was obvious that this was the most neglected of any room in the house. The once grand four-poster bed, hung with equal amounts of ragged bedclothes and spider webs, stood forlornly in the center of the room. It was flanked by delicately carved bedside tables, each blanketed with dust and topped with a grayed and filthy lamp and twin miniature portraits in tarnished frames. A vanity table and tiny chair were set along the wall opposite the bed.

A clear-thinking woman would have righted herself, dusted the filth from her clothes, and returned to work elsewhere. But the clouds of dust and dirt did little to quash my insatiable curiosity. Accustomed to these signs of neglect, I carried on with my exploration.

The overall air of the room, from the faded claret-colored bedcoverings and draperies to the petite vanity covered in an assortment of combs and pins, indicated a female occupant. To whom could it have belonged? I could no sooner picture a woman as a permanent resident in this isolated environment than I could a young child. What woman would willingly choose this as her home?

In the closet, alongside well-worn work garments, hung a number of lovely gowns. Itching to run my fingers over the rich fabrics but afraid of soiling them further, I gingerly touched the forgotten brushes, earrings, and pins littering the vanity table instead. Clearing the grime from a gilt-edged mirror, I imagined the young woman who might have tended her hair and checked the state of her frock here. Fragmented images drifted back to me of a distinguished young lady readying herself for an exciting evening at a mirror not unlike this one.

Using my already dingy apron, I cleaned the small picture frame from the closest bedside table and looked into it. The very face I had been imagining gazed back at me. I gasped. The same bright brown eyes set in a rounded face, complete with a pert chin and an enchanting smile.

Rose, the room seemed to murmur. A shiver ran up my spine.

How could this be? I had been dreaming of the woman for weeks. How could she be anything more than a figment of my imagination? Trembling, I rounded the bed and reached for another tiny portrait. I wiped it clean. A serious young man with straight black hair falling over a strong brow looked up at me. He was tall and solidly built, formal clothing outlining the breadth of his shoulders. Instead of the bronzed complexion one might have expected from someone of his stature, he was fair, with a graceful, long face and starry eyes. His lips curved up in the gentlest of smiles. I couldn't draw my eyes away from his. I felt my heart thump heavily. He was the man I had dreamed of since girlhood: tall and robust but with a certain sensitivity etched into his features. Judging from his clothing, he was obviously a gentleman. This made him, in a word, ideal.

I will keep my Rose here . . . The words echoed in my mind, bringing with them forgotten flashes of that first dream: a dazzling smile spreading slowly over a handsome face, a deep voice murmuring softly, and strong arms wrapped around me, creating a place of peace, security, and love.

Falling in love with a man like him would be child's play. Now that he had become more than a character in my dreams, I was half in love with him already. *He made a place for Rose*, I reminded myself, my throat tightening. *He was hers.* That realization was more than I could bear. How would I ever win someone like him stuck in a place like this? I glanced around the room once more, aching with loss. Even as derelict as the room was, it was more beautiful than anything I had ever had.

I quickly ducked out the door, closed it firmly behind me, and dropped the tapestry back into place. I pushed thoughts of Rose and her love from my mind, wishing to erase them and the melancholy that blossomed in my breast whenever I thought of them. I turned my mind to housework, burying my thoughts and feelings in menial tasks.

The afternoon I spent furiously cleaning and cooking kept the happy pair of lovers from my thoughts, but no amount of wishing could prevent my dreams from carrying me back to them while I slept.

Sitting before the glass once more, a lovely heart-shaped face gazed back at me, her brown eyes glowing. I fastened the rose-embossed locket around my throat and hurried from the room, my golden gown shushing pleasantly. My feet and heart were light as I made my way down the staircase, deliberately slowing my pace as I neared the last curve, dropping my lashes to cover the excitement in my eyes. I was greeted by a quick intake of breath as I rounded the last turn and emerged at the bottom of the stairs.

"Rosalind." My name was like a caress on his lips. His eyes shone with admiration as he took in every inch. "My lovely Rose, you are more beautiful that I could have imagined."

Unable to stop myself, I spun around, showing off the costly gown. "Do you like it? Truly?"

"No," he responded, shaking his head. Alarmed, I glanced up at him and was relieved to see his lips curve into the smile he saved just for me. He stepped forward and bowed, sweeping my hand to his lips. Looking up through dusky black lashes, he placed a kiss on my palm and said, "I love you, Rose."

My heart banging traitorously in my chest, I awoke, tangled in the emotions of the dream. Forcing my breathing to slow, I readied myself for the day. *Rosalind. Rose.* She was the girl who lived in my dreams, but she was also the girl from the portrait in the hidden bedchamber. The question rang in my mind: *What happened to her?* Somehow my destiny seemed interconnected with Rosalind. Her nearly tangible presence loomed over me. No matter what the cost, I had to know her fate.

Heading down to the kitchen, I considered how this might be best accomplished. My relationship with the Beast was tenuous, and any reference to the past would be met with stony silence at best. The only person I could turn to was Jack. The moment had come to swallow my pride and pray that I had not soured him against me.

I schooled my emotions, mentally rehearsing the conversation as I completed my morning chores. Lunch came and went, and I still did not find occasion to speak with Jack. Contemplating how I would bring the interview about, I watched the Beast tend to his garden—a collection of flowers, herbs, and vegetables— easily observable from the kitchen window. Though it seemed a strange pastime for someone so surly and impatient, he seemed to enjoy it. With a few tools in his hands, Jack approached him and the two exchanged a few words before Jack crossed to the front entrance. A few minutes later, the noises emanating from the drawing room revealed that he had started repairing the drawing room ceiling. Suddenly anxious, I hazarded a glance out the window to be check that the Beast was still busy. Wondering how long I had before either man finished his job, I hurried to the drawing room, my cleaning cloth in hand.

Jack, perched on a ladder and inspecting the damage to the ceiling, looked down at me. His eyebrows rose in surprise. I couldn't blame him. Lately, when his duties had brought him indoors, I had done my best to keep our paths from crossing, even though my feelings of betrayal had long since faded. The exchange at the Beast's door had been the most we had spoken in weeks.

"Bella," he said, greeting me with a nod.

At least he hadn't tossed me out of the room. Just the same, I felt dismayed by the coolness of his welcome. I weighed my words, wanting to hide my disappointment and ease into the conversation gradually. "Good afternoon, Jack," I responded, turning my attention to dusting an already spotless lamp.

"You needn't clean up after me," he said, fixing his eyes on the brown-stained ceiling. "I assure you, I will leave everything as it is."

This isn't going well, I thought. In a matter of seconds he had practically dismissed me. Pooling my resources of manipulation, I tried a different tact. "It isn't that."

"No?" He glanced down at me, his brows tented.

Painting an expression of vulnerability over my face, I played on his kind nature. "I feel badly . . ." I wrung my hands anxiously. "I have been unfair to you. After all, you are the only one attempting to make my stay bearable."

He glanced away, avoiding having to admit all he had done on my behalf.

"Thank you," I said softly. He didn't reply. He kept his gaze glued to the job at hand and began to chip away at the discolored plaster. I gave him a minute to work before saying, "I was wondering if I might ask something more of you."

Jack's dark eyes flicked back to me. "Yes?" I had elicited little more than one-word responses so far, but it would have to do.

"I have barely been able to sleep," I said, squeezing my eyes closed and massaging my temples for effect. "I've been plagued with strange dreams."

"What type of dreams?" His voice was light and conversational, his hands busy above him.

"A young girl appears regularly in them—rather pretty, with long, dark hair."

Jack's hands paused for a moment, unnaturally still. "Your sister?" he suggested.

Quick to set him straight, I replied, "No. I've never met this girl before, but I see her over and over in my dreams. She seemed to live here once. Her name was Rose."

I waited for his response. "Little stock should be put in dreams, Bella," he said, keeping his eyes fixed on his work.

"That's what I have always believed . . . ," I trailed off. "But then I happened upon a disused bedchamber that belonged to a woman."

He froze, his hands poised above him and his eyes riveted on the plaster. The time had come to play the trump card. "I found a portrait of Rose on the bedstand."

A deep sigh shuddered through him, and his hands dropped to his sides. Slowly, he descended the ladder and turned to me, sorrow burning in his eyes. "It's not my story to tell, Bella."

I fought the urge to proclaim victoriously, "I *knew* it!" But that was not the way to win Jack's trust. My instinct told me the best approach was straightforwardness. Taking a steadying breath, I met his gaze. "If you played a part, Jack, then that makes it your story."

His lips pressed together. Taking more time than was necessary, he wiped his hands on a cloth pulled from his pocket. "I did know Rose," he admitted, nodding resignedly. "She was one of my closest friends."

And yet you never appear in my dreams, I thought. It was only Rose and the tall, fair stranger. "What happened?"

"She changed," he said. "She was no longer the happy creature I had known since youth. One day she was living here, a joy to all in her presence, and the next she was gone."

I wondered if he had loved her, if the handsome stranger had stood between Jack and the object of his affections. A pang of jealousy stabbed through me for the woman who'd held the love of two such men. Pushing aside my feelings, I urged him to continue. "She left with no explanation? Without warning?"

"There were signs of her discontent," he replied, his eyes downcast, "but nothing to warrant such a sudden departure."

"Did you do nothing to find her—to discover the reason for her change in behavior?"

"No," he said, a quaver in his voice. "We simply fell apart. Isn't that enough?"

We? Had the Beast been involved as well? Or did he come into the story later, after Rose had left? Questions flew through my mind, threatening to burst free. But Jack's face was closed, his eyes guarded. "I don't wish to speak of this any longer," he said with a note of finality. He ascended the ladder once more, sadness carved in each line of movement.

The morsel I chewed on only made me long for more. And though he hadn't said so, I knew I had been dismissed again. With growing frustration, I stared up at the Beast's servant, craving answers and longing for a real conversation instead of the reminiscences and daydreams that filled my hours. Something in the bow of Jack's shoulders, however, a weariness I had never seen before, prompted me to leave him well enough alone.

His voice halted me in the doorway. "Bella," he called over his shoulder. I turned back, surprised by the intensity in his face. It reminded me of our previous argument outside the Beast's bedchamber. Looking directly in my eyes, he said, "You will speak of this no more."

Seven

The story, meager as it was, troubled me. Like a puzzle, certain pieces fit together perfectly. A hazy image flitted through my mind of her lover's hands brushing hers as they tamped down earth around a small rosebush. My heart throbbed in remembrance of the intimacy of the gesture, so simple and familiar, but so full of meaning. One thing was certain: Rose had lived here once, happy and beloved.

Other pieces of the tale left me baffled. For some reason, the same dream fostered my urge to run as far away from the Beast as possible. These had been Rose's feelings, I suspected, and they had been powerful enough to ensnare me with their potency. The face of Rose's lover drifted into my mind—the long, slim oval framed by dark hair, the luminescent eyes radiating undying affection.

She changed, Jack had said. But what could have caused her to run away from a life with her devoted lover? And how did he play into Jack's story? My hands submerged in quickly cooling dishwater, I shifted from foot to foot and considered everything I knew about that nameless man. I came to one conclusion: he was my ideal, the epitome of all I yearned for. Swift on the heels of that revelation came the next question, followed by a crushing blow of disappointment: Where was he now?

With more questions than answers, Jack's story left something else burning inside me: a need to redress the wrongs of the past. My heart whispered that if I could make some sort of recompense, I might one day be able to earn the regard of a man like the one who had loved Rosalind.

"We simply fell apart. Isn't that enough?" The words echoed in my mind, as full of naked anguish now as when Jack had uttered them. The night of my frustrated escape came back to me, Jack's words snagging at my memory: *He needs you. Don't you understand? He's lost everything.* If the Beast had lost everything, did that include Rose?

Like a brilliant sunbeam cutting through the cloud-covered sky, I saw how broken they both were: the Beast, a slave to his past and a shell of whatever he had once been; and Jack, dutifully hiding his pain and burying himself in his work. Tenderness tinted my vision of them both, softening their rough edges.

If Rose's actions had affected them both so deeply, perhaps mine could rectify the situation. I had never imagined that my responsibilities might include anything more than physical renovations, but I could now see that any lasting improvement had to take root in a deeper place—in the hearts of those I served.

I had never before felt an overwhelming drive to fix the wrongs of the past. Right now, undoing the mistakes I had made with my family was beyond my control, but perhaps helping the Beast and Jack would bring me one step closer to them. A grin spread over my face as I considered the prospect of nudging both of my new acquaintances toward a better life. My goal would be to help them heal, but that didn't mean I couldn't have a little fun while I was at it.

Since the Beast's activities kept him indoors for much of the day, it was easier to approach him than Jack. I discovered that the Beast spent the majority of his time shut up in his book-lined study, poring over the heaviest, most boring-looking volumes he could find. His daily study habit addressed the lingering questions I had about the books scattered around his bedroom. Apparently, he was obsessed with them.

It was a comfortable room, the walls lined with towering shelves full of more dusty books than I could count. A broad, grimy fireplace boasted a surprisingly cheery blaze next to a couple of well-worn armchairs. The Beast's desk was situated across the room.

Under the pretense of banishing the dust and cobwebs from the walls and shelves, I gathered my wits and entered the Beast's study.

"What are you doing?" he snapped, warily eyeing the broom and dusting cloths in my hands.

Jack had been right, I thought, remembering how he'd claimed that the Beast treasured his privacy.

"Dusting, sir," I replied cheerily, propping the broom in the corner. "I would have thought it was obvious." My feigned deference couldn't hold back certain sentiments—they flew out of my mouth before I could even think.

The Beast glared at me. "Perhaps I like the dust."

"Looking at your surroundings, one could come to that conclusion." I arched an eyebrow at him. "Sir."

He waved a hand dismissively. "Fine. Do what you will."

Obviously he was not in the mood for conversation. No matter. The fact that he hadn't thrown me out of the room was miraculous. *Baby steps*, I reminded myself, and proceeded to thoroughly clean the room. Everything was going well until I came to the top shelf above the arm-chair he was occupying. Perched as I was on the edge of his desk, I couldn't see the rather ugly bust pushed all the way to the back of the shelf. Eager to finish the job and give the Beast his space, I reached as far as I could and hastily swept across the shelf, catching a corner of the fragile bust and sending it crashing to the ground. It narrowly missed braining the Beast.

"Bella!" he roared, leaping from his chair, startled and enraged all at once.

I crouched to clean up the mess, brushing the frag-ments of the shattered bust into a pile. "I'm sorry," I said hurriedly, "I didn't mean to—"

"I don't care what you meant to do!" he bellowed, looming over me. "That was a family heirloom!"

Even in my terrified state, scrabbling in the dust at his feet for shards of plaster, I ruefully wondered if it was *his* family. I had only caught a glimpse of the bust as it came crashing down, but I had noticed how unsightly it was. But with him glowering down at me like a storm cloud, I knew that now would be a poor time to point this out. After all, I was in the wrong, and if I ever hoped to make things better, I needed to remember it.

"Maybe I can fix it?" I offered meekly, glancing up at him.

His eyes were wrathful. "I don't appreciate clumsy girls taking over my study!" he shouted. Then he stormed from the room, banging the door like a thunderclap as he went.

Trembling, I finished cleaning up the mess. *Well done, Bella*, I chided myself, vowing to take more care in the future when I invaded his sanctuary.

The inspiration for my next ploy came from my sister, Cassandra. With an unnatural amount of foresight, Cassie had packed a small sewing kit with my things. It contained little more that the basics: scissors, thread, and a tiny cushion loaded with needles and pins. While I fingered the small silver scissors and the spools of bright thread, I thought of Cassie and wondered how she might handle the situation with the Beast. Her approach was always direct, but no matter how difficult the challenge might be, she met it with tact and gentleness. Gathering up the small kit and a worn drapery, I reminded myself to speak as kindly as possible and made my way to his study.

Sewing in the evening required a place with adequate lighting, which meant the Beast's study. The idea of curling up in an overstuffed chair with my hands full of quiet work was unbelievably appealing after a day of sweeping and scrubbing. If entering the space put me in a position to begin goading the Beast toward betterment, what harm was there in that? After all, he had practically shoved me in that direction himself.

"What are you doing here?" He glared up at me from his desk when I entered with the mending. "You're blocking my light." From him, it was tantamount to a welcome.

"Pardon me," I replied tartly, already losing the battle with my tongue. "But since *someone* is too frugal to light the rest of the house in the evening, you'll have to endure my presence."

He mumbled something under his breath, turning his attention back to the vast tome before him.

"What are you reading?" I asked, easing into an armchair nestled beside the low-burning fire.

"Something I'm sure you'll enjoy," he muttered flatly, refusing to look up from the pages.

"I'm certain I shall," I returned, undaunted by his surliness. It was as much a part of the way he communicated as that horrid laugh of his.

"Agriculture," he said. This was also a characteristic of his communication style; any inquiry was met with the shortest possible response.

I was no more interested in agriculture than I was in learning how to milk cats, but I persisted because I couldn't resist bothering him while he was reading. "And what have you learned so far?"

"That certain young women are relentless pests," he responded blandly, his eyes still fixed on the book.

"Ridiculous," I chided. "That has nothing to do with agriculture."

And so it went. I needled, and he responded in kind. By the end of the evening, a sort of mutual respect had developed between us. It was better than before, when the Beast could hardly endure my presence and each encounter ended in one of us vacating the premises under extreme duress.

"I propose a compromise," I said, when the evening was drawing to a close. "I will do my best not to try your patience"—*what little you possess*, I added to myself—"if you allow me a place in your study."

"And you promise to do the dusting when I'm not present?" The gleam in his eyes was strangely teasing.

"Naturally."

He closed the book before him with a loud thump. "Fine."

Since establishing a relationship of any kind with the Beast was the crucial first step to setting my plan in action, I was content with the outcome. We weren't exactly friends, but at least we were mutually tolerant.

A succession of similar evenings followed. When I realized I was on solid footing, I made my next move.

"What is it now?" he demanded, his eyes never wavering from a volume as dull-looking as the one on agriculture. I had been staring disconcertingly at his blackened claws propped on the yellowing pages and his long, matted hair falling around his face. It was the type of visage that encouraged townsfolk to take up torches and pitchforks.

"Nothing," I replied innocently, shifting my gaze back to the crocheted mantelpiece I was repairing. I had planned this onslaught ages ago, and I had been waiting for the perfect moment to pounce.

"It's never 'nothing' with you, Bella," he said, my name little more than a growl at the end of the sentence.

I hesitated before speaking. "I was merely wondering . . ."

"Yes?" His tone was edged with impatience, his hard eyes flicking to mine.

"I wondered why you needed a servant at all. You already have Jack."

He looked at me as if I was mentally deficient—a look I was well acquainted with. "Yes. He's quite the house-keeper." he replied dryly.

"Maybe not," I said, pausing. The whole interchange had to feel unrehearsed, no matter how many times I had actually gone through it in my mind. "Then it stands to reason someone was needed to make improvements in your home."

His steely gray eyes narrowed, suddenly suspicious. He behaved like an animal at times, but in reality he was far too sharp for his own good. The best course of action was to get the whole thing out before he had a chance to guess what was coming. "Someone who has proven herself capable in one area might prove indispensable in another."

"What do you want, Bella?" I sensed the wariness in his tone. It reminded me instantly of my father. He also grew weary when I took too long getting to the point.

"I was just trying to help with the . . . smell." I uttered the last word quietly.

He rolled his eyes. "The house is spotless, Bella. What is left to smell?"

I lowered my gaze and stooped my shoulders, as if I was afraid to speak.

"Bella . . ." It was the way parents speak to naughty children, drawing out their names and punctuating them with a note of disapproval.

"It's you," I said to the damaged mantelpiece in my hands.

He emitted a huff of annoyance and pointed one claw toward the door. "Out."

Not wanting to push my luck, I methodically gathered my things and made my way to the door, careful to conceal my alarm. Might he actually murder me in my sleep? Perhaps he had never gotten over the incident with the bust. Hurrying to my room, I bolted the bedroom door just in case. My hands shaking only slightly, I pressed a chair under the knob. Better to be safe than sorry.

Later, tucked up in bed, I listened to the Beast bellowing incoherently while Jack lugged sloshing buckets up from the kitchen, and I smiled to myself.

His smell was intoxicating. Everything else—the time and place—was swallowed up when he was near. Closing my eyes, I leaned into him, breathing in the crisp outdoorsy scent and losing myself for a moment. The aroma reminded me of green growing things and crackling fires on cool nights.

Part of me insisted that I step back, arguing that this behavior was unseemly in a lady. Another part, the portion controlled by baser drives, savored the closeness of him and reveled in the fact that his aroma clung to my skin after we danced together.

Or kissed.

"Rose," he said, drawing me from my reverie. I cracked open an eye, catching the tiniest of smiles dart across his lips. We were spinning across the dance floor, inseparably connected. A couple as well paired as we were could not miss a step, even with our eyes closed. "What are you doing?" He sounded amused.

"Basking in the moment," I replied, my eyes half-lidded and my voice dreamy.

"Shall I join you?" he asked, slowing our movement and bringing our bodies closer until only a whisper separated us, our lips a tantalizing inch apart. At this proximity, his scent was overwhelming. Unable to stop myself, I reached up to clasp my hands around his neck and pull him to me. Our lips met. I luxuriated in the feel of his mouth on mine, soft and demanding at the same time, answering a need, a desperate yearning within me.

"Philip." The word was a half breath, half sigh that escaped me as our lips parted.

"Yes, my love?" he said, his voice husky and his breath slightly ragged. Pressed against his chest, I felt his heart race, mirroring mine.

"I think I adore you."

The sheets twisted about me as I fumbled in the dark for him. Reality rushed back to me as I realized where I was—alone in the Beast's home. My heart sank. It had only been a dream, though more captivating than the others had been. I disentangled myself from the bedclothes, tossed them aside, and lay on my back. Staring up at the ceiling, I allowed the cool night air to flow over me while I drew in long, calming breaths.

Fit the pieces together, Bella, the voice at the back of mind urged. All I wanted to do was curl up under the blankets and wallow in loneliness, but I forced myself to view the images analytically. *Rose loved Philip. Whatever else had happened, she truly loved him.* A circle of warmth spread over me at the name: Philip. If I knew nothing more of him, at least I knew his name.

With the Beast on the right track, Jack was my next project. The next day, I met him at the stable door with a cup of cool water. Ordinarily, I wouldn't have been caught anywhere near there on cleaning day—even with all my newfound experience in housecleaning, nothing could induce me to participate in mucking out the stable. But as Jack regularly spent the entire morning cleaning the stalls and replacing the soiled straw with fresh, I had to venture into unpleasant territory to seek him out. I had worked everything out beforehand. After thinking back on all the things he had done for me, I had surmised that the way Jack expressed regard for others was by serving them, and not just in the usual ways. He demonstrated respect by spending years at the side of a bad-tempered Beast and drawing baths for a serving girl that no one cared about. That was Jack. It stood to reason that if I wanted to win his affections, I should do the same for him.

"I thought you might like a cool drink," I said, passing it to him. I forced a gentle smile while trying not to breathe in the odor of animals too deeply.

He squinted at me half-suspiciously but downed the water just the same. "Thank you," he said politely, returning the cup to me. He wiped his brow, then placed an arm casually over the stable door and leaned on it. The gesture reminded me of Aaron so forcefully that I barely registered that Jack had asked me something.

"Pardon?" I brushed the memories of my lanky brother laboring in his workshop aside to focus on the present.

"I asked what brings you out this morning, Bella." His dark eyes were on me, carefully gauging my response.

I cleared my throat. "You've been working in the stable all morning, and I thought you might welcome a short break and a cool drink." I lifted up a saucer. "And some fresh bread."

He eyed the thick slice of bread, which I had smeared with ample amounts of butter and strawberry preserves. Learning to make my own bread had been tricky, but I was finding that as with everything else, where I persisted, I was successful. It had been fortunate, because Jack, I'd discovered, had a weakness for it.

He pulled a cloth from his pocket and wiped his hands before taking the plate from me. Swinging the door open, he stepped out, two frisky dogs barreling between us as he did so. "Don't mind them," he said as they careened around me before chasing one another across the yard. Turning back to Jack, I found him seated comfortably under a shade tree. He patted the spot beside him. "If you don't have to be back, sit with me for a moment."

I obediently sat beside him on the grass, tucking my skirts around me.

He gazed steadily at the bread on the plate, watching the butter melt down the sides. I could tell he wanted to shove the entire piece into his mouth, but he restrained himself. Warm bread fresh from the oven was his favorite, but from the uneasy expression on his face, I could tell that something else was on his mind. He carefully placed the plate on the ground and met my gaze. "I want to apologize for my conduct when you asked me about Rosalind. It was unforgivable."

This was something I hadn't anticipated. Leave it to Jack to say exactly what I was on the point of saying. I smothered my surprise and launched into my own apology. "I'm at fault, Jack. If I had realized the impact my questions would have had on you, the impact Rose had on this household, I would have stifled my curiosity." It was almost true. I would have stifled my curiosity until a more opportune moment. But the words had the desired effect—the crease between Jack's brows softened, and his eyes grew less troubled. "I do want to thank you, though, for helping me understand the situation. And I promise not to ask another question about Rose." *For now*, I mentally amended.

Relief flooded his face. "Thank you, Bella," he said, his gaze shifting to the thick slice of bread before him, his mouth likely watering over the thought of its buttery goodness.

"Of course, Jack. Now eat your bread before it gets cold."

That was just the first of many times I met him while he was working. I brought him treats from the kitchen and kept him company. I offered my assistance in washing the dogs, brushing down the horses, and passing him the tools for whatever repair he was making. Working side by side, we chatted amiably, and the instant friendship I had felt at our first meeting finally came to fruition. Jack became more like himself—cheerful and comradely. It was both comforting and encouraging.

Weeks after my first trip to visit Jack, I congratulated myself on a job well done while tackling the kitchen floor with a scrub brush. A warm hand settled on my shoulder, dragging me back to reality. The brush stilled as I looked up to see Jack beaming down at me approvingly.

"How did you do it, Bella?"

"It's a simple matter of employing a brush properly," I said, pushing an errant strand of hair out of my eyes. "Really, Jack, leaving a floor clean isn't that mind-boggling."

He rolled his eyes. "You know what I mean," he said, looking pointedly out the window to where the Beast tended his plants.

I pasted a serious expression onto my face. "My potent powers of persuasion, I suppose. I'm planning to use them on you as well."

Jack raised his hands to ward me off. "I don't need any of your special attention, Bella."

Too bad, I thought, suppressing a grin. *You're getting it anyway.* My approach with Jack was more aboveboard than it had been with the Beast, but I exercised my feminine wiles on him just the same.

"But I appreciate what you're doing for him," Jack said, giving my shoulder a small squeeze.

"It will take time to make a real difference," I said, studying the figure in the garden. It would take time to help them both heal from their past wounds. At least the first part had gone well; the Beast was clean, and Jack was on my side. It gave me hope.

"All good things do," Jack replied, a certain wistfulness settling over his features as he watched the Beast. The image of another boy wearing the same expression flashed through my mind. Almost as if he heard my thoughts, he said softly, "I'd give anything to have my friend back."

Standing up to fix my gaze on the master of the house, I wondered if the serious boy in the picture shoved to the back of Jack's dresser drawer could be the Beast. It would explain so much: why Jack had refused to leave his side; why they were both so damaged by past disappointments. Nothing of the pensive child could be found in the gruff creature, but there was no telling how life could change a person.

Behind me, Jack let out a deep sigh, pulling me from my contemplations. It didn't matter who the Beast was, I decided. Whatever the nature of their relationship, both of them needed me. It was somehow reassuring.

Eight

*T*he Beast had been maintaining better hygiene for a couple of weeks now, and as I stared at the long claws curling over the book in his lap, I decided that it was time to take his transformation to the next level. I cleared my throat and he glanced up, his eyes apprehensive. After the conversation about his smell, I could tell he was wary of what I might try next. I had been deliberately cautious to avoid a relapse.

"That looks like an interesting book," I commented, setting my mending in my lap.

"It's not full of fairy stories. You wouldn't be interested." His voice was low; he kept his eyes trained on the page.

"I might surprise you," I replied. "My interests are quite diverse."

He snorted. "It doesn't have anything to do with shoes, clothes, or jewelry either, if that's what you mean."

Seeing my in, I straightened my spine and lifted my

chin. "There's nothing wrong with being concerned with clothing and shoes. The right ensemble lends one an air of poise and refinement."

"Which is important to . . . ?" he asked, gesturing to the empty house surrounding us.

"It should be important to you," I supplied. "You are the master of this house, and as such, you have a responsibility to maintain a certain level of decorum."

He looked down at himself, taking in the tattered clothing he always wore, and shrugged.

I couldn't help myself. "It doesn't bother you that you look like some type of homeless animal—a crotchety bear trained to wear trousers?" His eyes narrowed, glinting in the light.

I examined my nails and added in an undertone, "And not even nice trousers at that."

"No, Bella. It *doesn't* bother me." The hardness of his tone and the sight of his hands tightly gripping the book contradicted his assertion.

This is too easy, I thought. Now to goad him in the right direction—without making him so angry that he'd throw me out on my backside, of course. "Are you sure you didn't escape from the circus?" I carried on. "Anyone who got a look at those bear claws of yours would surely die of horror."

His whole body stilled. Only his eyes moved, flicking to mine. "Claws?" The word was cold, quiet.

I refused to be frightened. "For lack of a better word, yes."

He glared down at his fingers and curled them into his palms. Rage radiated off him in waves.

"Perhaps if you took some hedge clippers to them, you could get them under control," I suggested. *You're poking the bear*, my conscience warned.

He turned his anger on me. "Why do you care?" he snapped, fury flashing in his eyes, revealing the pain behind it.

In that moment, I thought of my father. Though he was a mere carpenter, he was also a man who, like the Beast, valued the written word. We'd spent many nights like this—Father bent over whatever book he had borrowed from a neighbor, and me needling him for whatever I wanted most at the moment. He became irritated when I pushed him too far. Perhaps this similarity between the two men was my inspiration for what I did next. I discarded the notion of helping the Beast the way I saw fit. *Cassie*, I silently called out to my sister, *help me*. A memory flashed through my mind of Cassie calming my father's raw nerves after I had provoked him. Her kind eyes intent, she had looked into his and spoke the truth plainly and simply, infusing every word with love and respect. Summoning the courage to answer the Beast honestly, I said, "I'm sorry. I didn't intend to cause offense with my teasing." I prayed he could sense the sincerity in my tone. "The truth is that I'm puzzled."

"So I'm just a curiosity to you?" His words were clipped and angry. He was not one to be easily swayed.

I sighed, searching for the right words. "It isn't that. I just don't understand you at all."

"What's to understand? You said it yourself: I'm a *beast*." The words were no more than bravado hiding the hurt inside. I could see that now.

"There's more to you than that. I know it," I said, addressing the wounded child instead of the angry man. *The truth*, Cassie's voice seemed to murmur. *Have the courage to speak the truth.* I forced my mouth to form the words, remembering to speak as kindly as possible. "Why would you do this to yourself?"

"Maybe it wasn't a choice."

I smiled grimly, remembering how my own life had taken a turn for the worst. I had lost everything, yet I was making the choice to move forward. If I could find the strength to do so, then he could too. "We always have a choice. If nothing else, we can choose to accept the course life has set for us and make the best of it."

"You know nothing about me." The words were bitter, just as they had been when I'd expressed a similar sentiment to him. It was the same argument, our roles reversed. And now it was my turn to spell out the truths I knew about him.

"You've been hurt by things in your past. You were different before—better, maybe. But now you're stuck somewhere between man and beast in this half-life where you can never move forward. You must let go of the past and embrace the future that's waiting for you."

My frankness seemed to reach him at last. The anger drained from his face, revealing the weakness he tried so hard to hide. *We aren't that different after all*, I reflected. *We're both trying to hide who we are.* I watched him for a moment. His eyes were downcast, his bent frame emanated hopelessness, and something beyond pity or sympathy nestled in my heart—a mirror of what he was feeling at that moment.

"What if there's nothing better?" he asked huskily, his eyes never wavering from the floor. "What if it's too late and there's no going back?"

Unable to stop myself, I slid from my chair to kneel before him. My hand twitched at my side. I pictured Cassie placing a reassuring hand over Father's, but something inside me held back. *Those claws*, a voice in my mind muttered in disgust. Hesitatingly, I lifted a hand and placed it on his knee. Then, I looked up into his face and the words came easily. "There *is*. I can see the person inside you waiting to be free. Don't you think he deserves a chance at life and happiness?"

His whole frame shuddered as a deep sigh shook his body. He met my eyes. Then he nodded mutely.

The Beast's nails, neglected so badly they had grown thick, ragged, and almost beyond my ability to remedy, presented quite a challenge. I nearly sent Jack for the hedge clippers several times over the next few days. But several hours of hard labor produced a set of clean, manicured fingernails. *Perhaps there really is a man under all that filth and fur*, I thought, examining his large, capable hands.

The battle we had over his toenails, which were as appalling as his claws had been, was worse.

"When was the last time you removed your boots?" I asked, pinching my nose with one hand and holding the boots at arms' length with the other. Gagging on the pungent smell, I carried the boots a safe distance away and considered setting them on fire. *That would only smell worse*, a knowing voice informed me.

"I do bathe," he retorted.

"And who do you have to thank for that, I wonder?"

He narrowed his gray eyes at me. "Jack."

"Hmph." I crossed my arms over my chest. "If that's so, he should have given greater attention to your feet." I looked down at them. I didn't want to inspect them too closely. The stench had not come from the boots alone.

"Talking about me again?" At this point, Jack joined us, as he always did, seeming to sense that the Beast's patience with me was flagging.

Or mine with him.

Jack placed an arm around my shoulder and looked down at the Beast's feet. For a man who dealt with animal feces in all forms the expression on his face was quite appalled. "I'm not to blame for those."

The feet themselves were bad enough, hairy, large, and in need of a good scrubbing, but the yellowed and cracked toenails hanging far past the tips of the toes were more disconcerting.

"Hedge clippers?" I muttered to Jack.

"Absolutely."

A low growl emanated from the Beast. "I hate you both."

Several towels, buckets of hot water, a series of tools not meant for use on a human (I suspected they were for shoeing horses), and a great deal of growling, issuing threats, and howling in frustration—only part of which came from the Beast—and we were successful. His feet would never be attractive, but at least they were no longer unsightly.

In addition to doing away with the offensive boots, Jack was instrumental in selecting clothing from the Beast's closet, which I carefully mended until they resembled something suitable for a landowner. Pleased, I presented the outfit to the Beast. He took one look at the ruffled cuffs on the shirt and announced, "I'm not wearing that." Recognizing the I-refuse-to-be-persuaded stance—arms folded tightly over his chest and his eyes unyielding—I sighed, ripped off the ruffles, and resewed the cuffs.

Each piece of clothing gave rise to similar arguments, and in the end, Jack and I had to physically wrestle him into the whole outfit. Garbed in the redesigned white shirt, a carefully tailored jacket, an elaborately tied cravat, dark-colored breeches, and painstakingly shined knee boots, he almost looked human.

He glared at his reflection in the mirror, apparently unimpressed. "I look ridiculous," he muttered, and I caught something more about bears and trousers. Turning his irritation on me, he grumbled, "Why did I allow you to do this?"

I laughed aloud. "Allow me? Did you really think you had any choice in the matter?" His eye began to twitch, and his well-cared-for nails dug into his palms. He looked about to explode. I hastened to placate him. "You're quite right, though; something is definitely off about it." I stood beside him, gazing at his reflection and tapping my chin pensively, pretending to wonder what it was. From the neck down he could have passed for a tall, broad-shouldered, slim-hipped gentleman—country gentry, to be sure, but nonetheless respectable. However, the long, tangled rattails hanging about his face and obscuring his features could never be regarded as anything but disreputable. Unwilling to address the issue while he was still fuming over the clothing, I patted him on the arm consolingly and said, "I'm sure we'll figure it out tomorrow. Are you ready for dinner?"

"Get that thing away from my head." The Beast's teeth were clenched, and his words were muffled under all that hair, but the sentiment was clear enough. After hours of trying to comb through the tangled locks, I had made little headway, and the Beast was quickly losing patience.

So was I.

"Stop acting like a child!" I barked back, smacking him soundly on the head with the comb. The Beast rubbed the spot, glaring up at me like a wounded toddler. "Perhaps if you had taken a comb to this rat's nest in the last ten years, we wouldn't be having this problem!"

Without a word, the Beast snatched the comb from my hand and deftly snapped it in two.

"That's it," I said, extending my hand to Jack. "Shears!" I demanded. Jack wavered for a second, his eyes shifting back and forth between us, unsure of who was more dangerous. Deciding it was the woman with the mad gleam in her eye, he passed the scissors over.

"Noooooo!" the Beast protested, covering his head with both hands and slumping down in the chair.

"You leave me no choice!" Planting my hands on the arms of the chair he was sitting on, I bent forward until my face was inches from his. "Now, you can either act like an adult and allow me to remedy the situation, or I can have Jack physically restrain you."

His eyes darted to Jack, who looked taken aback for

a moment before matching the Beast's steely gaze with his own. A silent war waged between them. At last, the Beast tore his eyes from Jack, whose face beamed with victory. "Fine," he growled, removing his hands from his head. "But mind the ears. I don't fancy losing them to your vindictiveness."

"Manners," I said in a singsong voice. I waved the shears under his nose. "Remember who has the scissors."

The Beast merely groaned, clearly wondering how he had gotten himself into this mess.

I had watched my sister, the woman of many talents, skillfully cut my brother's and father's hair. Aaron favored a modern style, close-cropped on the sides and slightly longer on top, while my father preferred his softly wavy hair to cover his brow and neck. No matter which style she was undertaking, Cassie would snip cautiously until both parties were satisfied.

It quickly became obvious that either I lacked Cassie's skill or the challenge was too great for anybody. In the end, no one was satisfied. The Beast's hair had been impossibly snarled to begin with, and chopping it off had been the only viable solution. So I liberally hacked at the twisted locks until a pile littered the floor. Without the bulk of the tangled locks, the Beast's head looked smaller, and his well-shaped ears were now clearly visible. I stared at them thoughtfully for a moment, wondering what else lay concealed beneath his off-putting demeanor.

"Not the ears," he warned threateningly. The Beast,

though currently looking less beastly, seemed reluctant to discard his customary brusqueness. I turned his head to take one last snip at a long strand of hair in the front and found his gray eyes staring stormily into mine. Slim eyebrows winged above them where I had anticipated thick brambles. Incredibly long, black eyelashes, once veiled by masses of hair, ringed what I now realized were the most expressive and beautiful eyes I had ever seen. They were filled with a rare mix of emotions—the most prominent being annoyance. But it was countered, strangely enough, by a measure of thoughtfulness and the smallest amount of what almost seemed to be nervousness. A squirmy feeling took root in my breast. The world I viewed one way had tilted, surprising me with a new vista. What if the creature I had seen as nothing more than a beast stepped forward as a gentleman? Could I live with myself for how I had treated him? I swallowed hard and dragged my gaze from his, ill at ease with those light eyes boring into mine.

He patted his head with one hand, making sure his ears were intact. Then he surprised me by muttering a soft, "Thank you."

The squirmy feeling intensified. It felt as though a family of worms had taken up residence in my abdomen. I cleared my throat and made my tone light. "I've done all I can. It's your turn, Jack."

Jack, waiting beside me with a barber's accoutrements, went to work giving the Beast the first shave he'd had in years. I had originally offered my services, savoring the thought of taking a naked blade to the Beast's throat after all the fuss he'd made over his hair and clothing, but I had been voted down. Jack, much more gently than I would have done, worked to remove the years' growth of beard. The Beast seemed to relax at his hand, confident in the ministrations of his trusted companion.

My mind flitted over the experiences of the past months in the Beast's house as I watched them. I had finally been accepted—albeit begrudgingly—as a member of the household. Despite the Beast's initial impression of me as a no-talent, spoiled princess, I had become proficient at caring for his home and preparing his meals. I had gained some measure of his respect, and, in turn, confidence in my own abilities. Jack had stood beside me even when I refused to acknowledge his existence. I had come to rely on that support and companionship more than I cared to admit. He was the only real friend I'd ever had, and I found that friendship incalculably valuable.

It was strange—for the first time in my life, I was appreciated for what I had achieved and the person I had become, rather than for the impressive baubles and pricey finery I once donned. The feeling thrilled me. How odd that it had been brought on by such men.

Gazing down at my chipped nails and chapped palms, I felt more homely than ever, but somehow I was more at peace with myself as well. Meditatively, I fingered the jewel still at my throat. All my life I had assumed I was destined for wealth and power—a queen with the world at her fingertips. But destiny, it seemed, had another plan. Here I was only me, stripped down to the barest of essentials: a strong head, capable hands, and, perhaps for the first time, a good heart. If I, Beast-like, refused to discard certain undesirable personality traits—my sharp tongue, for instance—that was my prerogative. I was proud of who I had become.

"What do you think?" The pride in Jack's voice reflected in his beaming face. Motioning him aside, I saw the product of his efforts. Wearing the reddened cheeks of the freshly shaven, with broad shoulders hunched and beautiful eyes anxious, sat Philip.

My world shifted again, tipping and sliding until I lost my balance and tumbled. The floor rushed up toward me, the edges of my vision growing hazy. I wasn't sure I had really seen the Beast spring from his chair until I felt his arms close around me, catching me mid-fall.

"Bella!" His voice was filled with tenderness, so startling it kept me conscious a moment longer. Long enough to look up toward his face and see the ghost a second time.

"Philip," I murmured, and the world faded to black.

Nine

Someone gently caressed my hair where it spread across his lap. "Wake up, my sweet," he whispered, his breath tickling my ear.

Philip, *the wise voice in my mind supplied.*

"Mmmm . . . ," *I replied, far too comfortably curled against him to pay any heed.*

"If you don't wake up, I can't give you your present," *he coaxed.*

Now he had my attention. I opened my eyes halfway, looking up at him through long lashes. "Present?"

"Yes." He grinned.

"All right, but it had better be good." I sat up on the divan and did my best to suppress a yawn, anxious to know what he would give me.

He placed a finger under my chin, gently tilting my head up until our eyes met. "First, I want you to know how much I love you—how much I have always loved you," *he said earnestly. "You are everything I have ever wanted. That is why I want to give you this." He fumbled in his jacket pocket for a moment before a gold chain slid between his fingers, a large red pendant hanging from it. "I know it's customary to give the woman you love a ring, but this was my mother's." The jewel twisted and glinted in the air, capturing the afternoon light and sending it dancing over the walls. Unable to tear my gaze away, I stared at it, enraptured.*

"It's perfect," I said, *longing to run my fingers over its glittering facets.*

"Truly?" Eagerness spilled out of him; he looked like a little boy whose biggest wish had been granted. "You'll be my wife?" he said, throwing his arms around me and crushing me in an exuberant embrace. He must have felt me stiffen in his grasp because he pulled away, a hurt look scrawled across his face. The pendant slipped from his hand to rest on the divan between us.

Why are you pushing him away, you stupid woman? *the voice in my mind demanded.*

I rushed to reassure him, linking my hands with his. "Of course I'll be your wife."

Much better.

Visibly relieved, a grin began to creep over his face again.

"It's only . . . you didn't ask me to marry you," *I finished.*

His eyebrows rose, his gray eyes wide with alarm. "I didn't? But I thought—"

I placed a hand over his mouth, stopping him. Smiling as gently as I could, I said, "Do it now."

The voice inside me was silent, expectant.

Taking a bracing breath, he fell to his knees before me. His eyes focused on our interlinked fingers. Speaking slowly, he said, *"Will you take me with all my shortcomings and mistakes? Can you find it in your heart to love me anyway?"* He *turned those beautiful eyes, gleaming with pure love, on me.* *"Rosalind, most beautiful and wonderful of women, will you be my wife?"*

Rosalind? *the voice asked.* Rose, *it reiterated with a note of sadness.*

I leaned toward him, twining my hands in his hair and pulling his mouth to mine. When at last we parted, I brushed my lips over his ear to whisper, "Always and forever."

A hazy conversation pulled at me. Disembodied voices spoke in the dark, dragging me from wherever I had been. I didn't want to return; the pressure of Philip's lips on mine was the most delicious thing I'd ever experienced.

"How did she know my name? Did you tell her?"

"No, of course not. But she's known about Rose for some time. She says she's had dreams about her."

"Dreams? About Rose?"

"Yes."

"How is that possible?"

"I have no idea. It seems strange, but she knew a lot about Rose before she found the room. I'm sure that confirmed her suspicions."

Silence met this declaration. Then, "Is that when she came to you? What did you tell her?"

"Only that I knew Rose before she ran away."

"Nothing else? You didn't tell her—"

The voices rumbled on, but the thick darkness sucked at

me, muting the conversation. My mind filled with strange images of my family and my childhood home being buffeted by the worst storm I had ever lived through. The doorway was filled with a black shadow. *The Beast*, the voice whispered. I tried to make sense of the images. It hadn't been the Beast. It had only been my father.

The Beast. The word hissed through my mind. *Philip. Rose.*

The ruby lay cold against my chest as I thought of them. It was a constant reminder of the price my father had been willing to pay for me. Now I understood its significance as a symbol of the bond between Philip and Rose—a token of their engagement. The conversation tugged at me once more, drawing my attention away from the jewel.

"Will she be all right?" The voice was anxious but low, almost a purr. It echoed strangely against my ear, as if I was pressed to the speaker's chest.

"She's had quite a shock. Give her some time," a calmer voice advised, a flicker of concern wavering behind the composure.

I felt a hand gently patting my cheek. "Bella, please," the first speaker pleaded. "Come back to me." Something in me longed to comply, but another part of me, still aching from the vision that had just closed, didn't want to face reality yet.

"Perhaps if we throw some water on her . . . ," the second speaker mused.

Eyes still closed, I made my mouth form the words, "Not if you value your life, Jack." That sort of insolence couldn't be tolerated, no matter how much it cost me.

He chuckled. "She's perfectly fine."

I opened my eyes to slits, cautiously taking in the situation and trying to piece together what had happened before I'd lost myself to fractured dreams. I focused first on Jack, who was standing some distance away with a look of mingled relief and amusement on his face. Then, turning to gaze up at the Beast—*Philip*, the voice from my dreams corrected—I found myself cradled against his chest. I struggled to meld what I knew of the Beast and his history with the man who held me so gingerly in his arms. I felt my cheeks flush, embarrassed by the tenderness of the gesture, so out of character for the personage I knew as the Beast.

"Are you all right?" he asked, his light eyes tinged with apprehension. His voice was the same: low, gruff, and more used to growling than speaking softly. The same voice, bent in tender tones of affection, had begged for Rose's hand in my dream.

Rose . . . the voice hissed again.

Feeling like an intruder on her memory, I scrambled out of his arms and pushed myself into a sitting position a safe distance away. "I'm fine, thank you." It sounded strangely formal, especially since I'd just been nestled against his chest. My cheeks burned at the thought.

His eyes clouded with disappointment, and his brow furrowed. "I'm sorry, Bella. I thought you could only see me as—well, as a beast. I didn't know how to tell you the truth."

I brushed his comment aside with the wave of a hand and got to my feet, my knees slightly wobbly. "No matter. I think I'd like to rest, though." I cleared my throat. "It's been a . . ." I paused, searching for the right word. ". . . an enlightening day."

The Beast—Philip—remained on the floor, staring at his hands, as if noticing for the first time how empty they were. In the same instant, my shoulders felt cold.

Jack placed a hand on my elbow, steering me toward the stairs. "I think that's best, Bella. I'll see you to your room." We walked in silence. I was too shaken to speak, and Jack left me to my thoughts. He opened the door to my bedroom and stepped aside. Halfway across the threshold he gripped my arm, halting my passage. I glanced back at him.

"Are you all right, Bella? It's a lot to take in." Concern rang in his tone, his dark eyes intent.

Having come to trust him so implicitly, the truth spilled out before I could stop it. "I don't know." I ordinarily tried to hide the weariness in my voice, but this time it was audible. But this was Jack, and he would probably see through any ruse I put forward anyway. "Why didn't you tell me?"

One corner of his mouth pulled down, as if something didn't sit well with him. "I wanted to, Bella. But it wasn't my story to tell." Regret spread over his face. "I'm sorry."

"It seems everyone is sorry," I mumbled. The sadness in his eyes intensified, and my conscience panged. I forced a small smile. "You've done the most of anyone to help me understand things, Jack. I know that," I said. "It's been a difficult week for all of us. I'm sure everything will be normal tomorrow."

The gloomy expression lightened. "Yes, of course,

Bella. I'm sure you're right." He took his hand off my arm and moved to close the door, his eyes full of pity.

The four walls squeezed in on me. The bedcovers, far too hot, twisted around me and pressed the air from my lungs. I desperately threw them off and strode to the window, flung it open, and gulped in fresh air. Assuring the Beast—Philip—and Jack that I only needed to rest had been easy. Convincing my mind of the matter was proving impossible. It manically whirred from one image to another with increasing speed, mashing them into an incoherent jumble: Philip, stringing the red jewel around Rose's neck, his fingers lingering on her skin; the Beast, tossing me mercilessly to the floor, his eyes wrathful; Jack, his hand resting on my shoulder, smiling at me, his brown eyes full of approval; the Beast, now with Philip's face, cradling me in his arms and begging me to awaken; Jack, looking on as Philip and Rosalind tended the rose garden, wearing an expression of untold loss; Father, firm and disapproving, as I wheedled yet another expensive piece of clothing out of him; Aaron, his arms crossed over his chest, his eyes hard as he drove me from our home; Cassie, sitting beside her loom, covering her face with her hands, her whole body wracked with sobs. Finally, spinning over the dance floor, I was tucked tightly in the arms of a man whose face flickered between Philip's, the Beast's, Jack's, Father's, and Aaron's.

"Enough!" I said aloud, digging my fingers into the wood of the window frame until the pain chased their faces from my mind. My sanity was slipping.

I pushed free of the windowsill, propelling myself toward the door, slowing only to grab the thin robe from the foot of the bed, shove my arms into it, and tie it at my waist. Determined to reach the kitchen, I padded down the hallway. The escape route was all too familiar. As I reached the kitchen door leading outside, a dim reflection in the window caught my eye: a shapeless form of white robe and nightgown, the oval of a pale face above, dark wavy hair spilling about it, and a flash of wild eyes. Averting my gaze, I refocused on the door and carefully pushed it open. My unshod feet met cool earth as I sped over the grounds toward the stable. The slimmest band of light edged the eastern sky. I had spent the night in tortured ruminations, and now I sought to still them with blustering winds and the feeling of a horse beneath me. Straw scratched the soles of my feet, but I no longer cared about my own discomfort. I fumbled with the saddle, my hands shaking as I pulled it from its place on the wall.

"Let me help you with that." Firm hands settled beside mine, lifting the saddle from my grip. I turned and saw Jack. His eyes were black and unreadable in the dimness. Wordlessly, he saddled the horse while I looked on, shuffling my feet nervously. At last he slid the reins into place and glanced back at me. "So, where are we going?"

I summoned enough strength to reply, "Away."

The wind tugged at me, filling my nostrils with the aroma of late summer, whipping my hair and threatening to tear the flimsy robe from my shoulders. I leaned into

Jack's broad back, my hands clasped around his waist. He was the only thing anchoring me at the moment— the only thing keeping me from flying apart. His stability, his friendship, his kindness—without them, I would have been lost. As it was, holding onto him, allowing his warmth to seep into me, my head began to clear, and I felt more like myself.

I had expected an argument from Jack like we'd had the last time—a renewed refusal to let me leave. Instead, after readying his own horse, Jack mounted and pulled me up behind him, then worked the mount to a gallop while the house diminished to a speck behind us. Now we were practically flying across a wide meadow, our path marked only by the whispering grasses waving behind us. The wind tasted of freedom, and I sucked it in until its cold clutched at my lungs. Seeking warmth, I curled against the solidarity of the man before me, tucking my cheek against his back. The mount slowed, and Jack glanced over his shoulder.

"Cold?" he asked.

A sigh escaped me. Without the breeze to push away the unwanted images, they began to creep back, and like the sky above us, they grew brighter by the minute. In my mind's eye, I saw Philip sitting dejectedly on the floor, his eyes hollow and his hands empty. I met Jack's gaze, which was full of questions but held no hint of disapproval.

"We have to go back," I said finally.

A corner of his mouth lifted, in a half grin, I guessed, though only a sliver of his face was visible. "I thought you'd say that," he said, turning the horse back the way we'd come. The animal trotted unhurriedly along, my heart bumping against my ribs to the rhythm of its hoofbeats.

To distract myself from what awaited at the end of our journey, I launched into conversation. "Why didn't you stop me?"

A chuckle shook his frame. "If you could have seen yourself, you'd know why."

I glanced down at my bare feet, smudged with dirt. I probably did look rather desperate, but I had probably looked desperate the last time as well. "I was a mess before, and you had no trouble saying you wouldn't help me." I felt him let out a long breath.

"I could tell you'd had a rough night. When I saw you wander out here, I decided that the least I could do was make sure you didn't hurt yourself."

"Thank you," I whispered. I leaned against him and tightened my grip around his middle, trying to soak up all the solace afforded by his company. "Would you have let me run away this time?"

He didn't answer.

The sun had just peeked above the far-flung hills when we reined in before the house. I wasn't sure what kind of reception I'd receive and was surprised to see Philip sitting on the steps, his broad shoulders bowed and his head in his hands. He looked up as Jack swung me to the ground.

"I'll take care of the horse," Jack said quietly, turning the mount toward the stable before anyone could respond.

I stood before Philip, tugging at my thin robe in an effort to conceal the dingy nightgown beneath and all too aware of my grubby feet poking out below the hem. My wind-snarled hair and tired eyes undoubtedly betrayed a sleepless night.

Even garbed in yesterday's rumpled clothes, Philip was beautiful. The sunlight caught his dark lashes, casting shadows over his cheeks and making the lashes appear even longer. They lifted as his gray eyes pored over me.

"I thought you had gone," he said.

I shuffled nervously from foot to foot, unsure how to answer.

"I wouldn't blame you." His voice was low but softer, lacking its usual bravado. "You wouldn't be the first."

My heart melted, all embarrassment at my appearance forgotten in an instant. I saw again the damaged creature behind the Beast's rough façade, and I longed to offer him comfort. Sitting gingerly beside him on the step, I replied, "You could have told me about Rose. About you. About everything. I would have understood."

His face hardened. "How? 'Pardon my claws, but I look like an animal because I was abandoned by the love of my life'?" He shook his head and grumbled, "It isn't exactly dinner conversation."

"It sounds simple enough," I replied, looking over the grounds before us. "All girls dream about that, you know—the romantic gentleman who can't recover from lost love." After a moment, I added archly, "Mind you, no one expects a beast to be quite so sentimental."

He groaned, burying his face in his hands once more. "I'm a fool."

I remembered the vision of his proposal to Rose, and the words slipped out. "Do it now."

He looked over at me, confusion painting his features. "Do what?"

"Tell me everything."

Ten

*P*hilip began, hesitantly at first, to reveal his past. He and Jack had grown up together. Philip was the son of a wealthy landowner, and Jack was the son of his steward, but there was little distinction made between them. Whenever Philip was offered an opportunity in education or training, the same was extended to Jack. There were no mothers to insist that they assume their proper roles—Jack's had run away when he was young and Philip's had died in childbirth. Their fathers, both busy with their own affairs, couldn't be bothered to ensure a proper upbringing.

Beyond being thrown together by circumstance, the boys were naturally drawn to one another by temperament. Philip was the scholar and born leader, while Jack's easygoing disposition—paired with his staunch loyalty—guaranteed that he'd follow his friend into any adventure. They were a perfect pair of young miscreants before they met Rose.

On one of their many excursions, they encountered a young girl in the forest. She had been pretending she was ridding the kingdom of fire-breathing dragons. The boys soon learned that Rose preferred climbing trees and tracking animals to the more feminine pursuits of needlework and reading.

"She was lovely even then," Philip said. "All dimples and charm. It took her no time to get our approval. She batted her lashes at me and teased Jack, and she'd captured us."

They both adored her, I thought. Aloud, I asked, "Was she all alone?"

"Yes," he replied, his face taking on the wistfulness I remembered from the portrait in Jack's room. "She lived with an elderly grandmother who didn't attend to her much. Like Jack and me, she was given free rein for adventuring. Rose had an avid imagination, and she pulled us into her games of make-believe. We were lackeys to Her Highness, pirates to her pirate queen. Whatever she wanted, we did it."

Picturing the woman I had seen in my dreams as a little girl made me smile. Would I have liked her? My own sister had been sweet, but Cassandra was too overly serious and concerned with running the house to make a good playmate. I had never had a real girlfriend, and as I grew older, my ruthless ambition to catch men kept other women at a distance.

Oblivious to my mental meanders, Philip continued with his tale. "We spent every day together, playing, laughing, and exploring. Life was perfect." His face clouded for a moment. I held my breath to keep from hurrying him along. My curiosity was insatiable.

"Then," he continued at last, "Rose's grandmother passed away."

Now that he'd broached the subject, I hoped it would be like drawing a cork from a bottle, allowing the contents to finally flow free. If only I could keep him talking, I'd learn the whole story. "She had no other family?" I prompted, my heart sorrowing for the young girl left without kin.

"Yes," he replied. "Rose would have been sent to an orphanage. All three of us were devastated at the thought of being separated. I was ten, but I knew I loved her more than I had ever loved anyone. So, with Jack by my side, I went to my father and begged him to intervene on her behalf. Our pleading moved him, even though he had no clue how to raise a child—much less a girl—but he made the necessary arrangements for her care and provided a place for her in our home."

"So she became part of your family?" My mind jumped ahead, and I considered how strange it would be to fall in love with someone in your household. "Like a sister?"

I could tell by the flick of a glance he sent me that he knew what I was thinking. At least the uncanny powers of observation were something I could attribute to Philip, not just the Beast. "It wasn't like that. We lived in the same house and spent every day together, but the way I adored her as a boy grew into the love I felt for her as a man."

I plowed on, resolved to have all my questions answered now that he was willing to speak. "And Jack?"

He shot me another of those quick glances, as if I had caught on to something others typically missed. "Yes, he loved her too. In fact, after she came to live here, we regularly battled over whom she loved best." Recalling the silent war they'd waged when I'd tried to cut his hair, I believed him. Philip was well above average in stature making Jack the smaller of the two, but I didn't doubt his ability to teach his friend a lesson. "Sometimes it went his way, sometimes it went mine, but we both knew that Rose was strong-willed enough to make her own choice in the end."

"And she chose you?"

His eyes took on a faraway look as he remembered. "I was as surprised as anyone."

I thought I understood why Rose would prefer him to his friend, but my own feelings were so muddled with Rose's I couldn't be certain. So I asked, "Wasn't the relationship considered . . . inappropriate?"

"My father had passed away by then, and so had Jack's. The three of us were left to care for one another as well as the estate. There was no one left to disapprove, and after having grown up together, it wasn't peculiar to us. The place had a full serving staff then, which made it less unusual." His brow furrowed as if something had occurred to him, and I wondered if it was the same thought that had flashed through my mind: two men and one woman, alone like we were, but with the addition of a houseful of servants to make it proper. Forcibly, I reminded myself of my position. I wasn't a treasured member of the household like Rosalind; I was only a serving girl. Considerations for propriety were unnecessary.

In an effort to divert my mind from that train of

thought, I fired another question at him. "You fell in love each other just like that?"

He sighed, kneading his forehead with one large hand. "It happened over time, I suppose. So gradually I hardly noticed. I only knew I never wanted to be parted from her."

"What about Jack? How did he feel when the relationship between you and Rose became serious?"

"Jack . . ." His voice trailed off while he ruminated. "Jack bore things as he always did—with grace and good humor. I could never be sure if he loved her in a romantic way, but sometimes I caught him looking sad when Rose and I were together. That was all."

He buried himself in his work even then, I thought. Jack preferred productivity to wallowing in self-pity, and I admired him for it. He was not the type to let himself go to waste, no matter how heartbroken he might be. On the other hand, I could understand why Philip, with his sensitive soul, had taken that route. He felt things deeply, and once he had learned to love he clung onto it, even if it meant losing himself.

I had dreamed of such a man once, one who would pine for me in that way. Now my practical mind questioned the usefulness of putting one's life on hold for a dream. Strange that I should abandon the ideals I had always held dear, but my time here—learning to work, finding pride and purpose in labor, and winning Jack and Philip's friendship on my own merits—had transformed me. I was no longer the creature I had been when I had arrived. I rubbed the stone at my throat as I mulled it over. The motion drew Philip's eye.

"I gave that to her as an engagement present," he said quietly. "It used to be my mother's."

These details had been revealed to me in my dreams. But even though it might be odd to wear the jewel after I had discovered its history, the necklace provided a link to home and reminded me of all that my father had done for me. I reached up to unclasp it and return it to him, but he raised a hand to stop me. "Don't," he said. "It pleases me that you wear it."

I dropped the necklace back into place, regarding it meditatively. It occurred to me how strange it was that my father had come across the jewel in the woods, as if it had been carelessly discarded. If I found it to be so precious, why hadn't Rose?

"Why didn't she take it with her when she left?" I asked. It would have reminded her of Philip and the life she'd left behind, true, but it was beautiful and obviously costly, and if Rose had set out on her own, wouldn't she have taken it at the very least as insurance against poverty?

"I thought she had," he said, his eyes on the ruby at my throat. "Until the day your father found it." Looking him over, I wondered how the innate gentleness and romanticism of his youth had transformed into the coarseness that typified the Beast. As far as I knew, there had been no sign of the Beast in the younger man, no indication of what he would become.

"Something inside me . . . snapped." The last word was so quiet, so laced with chagrin, that I almost didn't catch it. But I knew what had happened next. My father's words haunted me, and even in the face of

Philip's obvious remorse, my ready temper flared as I remembered them.

"And you vented your anger at losing Rose on the first unsuspecting victim to come along?"

He buried his face in his hands once more, his dark hair standing out in a messy halo. The sight reminded me of a little boy crushed by a harsh reprimand.

Feeling like I'd abused a helpless creature, I took a deep breath and attempted to tamp down my anger. "I'm sorry," I said. "I spoke rashly."

He removed his hands, not bothering to smooth his hair back into place. "Why apologize? It's the truth," he said bitterly. Mouth set in a grim line and brow furrowed, he explained, "Seeing the jewel confirmed that Rose wasn't returning. I thought because she had taken it with her, it meant she still cared for me in some way. I believed that for seven long years. To see it cast aside like that, lying unwanted on the forest floor . . ."

"Was unbearable," I finished.

He nodded, his Adam's apple bobbing as he swallowed back his emotions. "I had already given in to grief. I let no one near me but Jack. And I became a beast." My heart flooded with guilt. If I had known him for what he truly was, I would never have called him that.

"When I saw your father holding the stone," he continued, "my last flicker of hope and humanity vanished."

Sorrow and loss can drive a person to many things. I recalled how Father yearned for my mother, refusing to even look at another woman. In his heart, he would always be faithful to his first love. Philip was the same type of man.

"You loved her," I said, putting my thoughts into words, "and when you realized she was gone, you lost sight of who you were."

"Perhaps," he relented. Then he continued dryly, "But I derived a certain amount of pleasure in making others feel as miserable as I did. It's the reason everyone left. Except Jack—he refused to be driven away."

I felt my lips curve into a small smile. That was Jack—fiercely loyal despite the circumstances.

"Then you came," he said gruffly, "turning everything upside down, nosing your way into our lives, and refusing to be cowed no matter how you were treated. It brought out the worst in me."

I flashed him a smirk. "I admit, I enjoyed provoking you. I needed to bully someone who wouldn't just lie down and take it."

"I hated you at first," he said. I wasn't surprised by that. "You were nothing like Rose. Hard where she was soft, harsh where she was gentle." He looked at me pensively, and that long look made me feel as if all my deepest, darkest secrets were on display. "But I realized I was wrong."

"Really?" I cocked an eyebrow. "Spoiled brat, entitled princess . . . it seems like you had me pegged from the beginning."

"I thought I did, but as one who's spent years hiding behind a rough exterior, I couldn't help seeing past yours."

I remembered how he—the Beast—had looked at me from time to time, a flash of understanding and sympathy in his eyes. It was a hallmark of Philip, though I had associated it with only the Beast till now. I doubted that even my family understood me as well as he did. An image of Aaron, stern and implacable as he drove me from my home, flashed through my mind as proof.

"You're quite like her, actually," he said, "in your strength of mind and your sense of purpose. That's what made me see the error of my ways. It helped me remember the person I once was."

"Thank you," I replied quietly, accepting the praise even though it left me ill at ease. I stared down at my grimy feet. *I'll never be as good and beautiful as Rosalind*, I thought, trying to tuck my toes beneath the hem of my soiled nightgown. Suddenly, I wanted this conversation to come to a close so that I could change into my workday clothes and distract myself from my shortcomings with some type of heavy housecleaning. One more question remained, though, and pulling myself together, I turned to face the man at my side. "What happened to her, Philip?"

"I don't know," he answered miserably. "Everything seemed fine. We were engaged to be married. The future was set. Then we quarreled over something—I can't even remember what. We had passed through so many difficulties together that it seemed insignificant. But in the morning, she was gone. She left many of her things behind, but those she treasured most were missing."

"She left no note? No word with one of the servants?" I asked. I needed to know what had happened to her. From what I knew of Rose, she wasn't the type to disappear without explanation.

"Nothing," he said, an echo of the desolation he must have felt ringing in his voice.

"Why didn't you go after her?" I asked in frustration. The fact that he had not attempted to follow the woman he loved bothered me nearly as much as the fact that she had run away from him in the first place.

"I was too shocked at first. Then, when no word of her came, my grief turned into anger and I became determined not to be the one to relent. Jack begged me to reconsider, and after a time, I gave him permission to do as he saw fit, but by then it was too late. All trace of her was gone."

Nothing could convey how I felt when he said those words. A mixture of pity, affection, and the urge—however impossible—to wipe the slate of the past clean buzzed through my veins. Noting the hopelessness on his face, I did the only thing I could. Leaning my head on his shoulder, I slid my hand into his, feeling his smooth, warm palm curve around mine. I never would have imagined that holding hands with the Beast would be like this, but I should have known from my dreams that Philip would have just the right type of hands for holding. Our fingers woven together and our words spent, we watched the morning blossom in silence.

Eleven

*N*o more than a pinkish haze beyond my eyelids for one blissful moment, the sun crept across the pillow to warm my face. I opened my eyes with a start. It was full day, and I had slept in. What had I been thinking? Who would do the chores? Who would set the bread and plan the men's meals? They would manage on their own, no doubt, but it was my responsibility. I hastened to throw on my serviceable dress and apron, but they were not on the chair where I had left them. In fact, upon closer inspection, the entire room was far more orderly than it had been yesterday. Just as I began to panic, a throat cleared behind me.

"Looking for these, my lady?"

I turned to see a young woman, no older than eighteen, standing at the foot of my bed and holding out a dress and stockings. Trying to keep my eyes from popping out of my head, I asked, "Who are you?"

"Penelope, miss," she replied with a prim curtsey. "I'm your lady's maid."

"Ummm . . ." Clearly I had heard her wrong. Either that or I was still dreaming. I pinched myself to be sure. *Ouch.* I was most definitely not dreaming. "Pardon me?"

"I'm your lady's maid," she repeated, her face dimpling at my confusion.

I tried another tact. "But where did you come from?" I certainly didn't remember having a maid before I went to sleep. Looking askance at the bed, I wondered just how long I had been out. A number of weeks, perhaps? A hundred years?

"I'm from the village, my lady. Master Jack hired me yesterday."

Master Jack, I thought, the deference in her tone drawing my attention. He had obviously been busy. Now that I was paying attention, the sound of other occupants in the house met my ears: subdued conversations, the scrape of furniture being shuffled from place to place, and someone humming merrily while sweeping the corridor. I refocused on Penelope.

"And which village would that be?" From time to time, I wondered exactly where my current home lay in relation to Stohl, but I had never asked. It might have been important if any of my escape plans had been successful.

"Stone, miss."

I had heard of Stone before. The same expansive woods that separated Stohl from Camdon on the north also separated it from Stone and several small communities on the east. Doing a quick calculation, I guessed that Stone was no more than a day's journey from my home, in good weather at least. Philip's home was probably about the same distance; after all, I had arrived in less than a day.

"May I help you dress for the day, my lady?" Penelope asked, interrupting my thoughts and once again holding out the clothing. Directing my gaze onto what she held in her hands, I realized it wasn't my work dress and heavy stockings after all, but a buttery yellow day dress and a pair of silk stockings.

"Those aren't mine," I said, eyeing them enviously just the same.

"Of course they are, miss. They arrived this morning, and I've only just finished pressing them." She grinned up at me again.

"Master Jack?" I asked.

"I assume so, miss."

Seeing that further inquiry was pointless, I allowed Penelope to help me into the clothing. The dress fit as if it had been made for me, as did the stockings and a new pair of fawn-colored ankle boots Penelope produced. I admired myself in the glass as Penelope twisted the front of my hair up, fixing it in place with an elegant flowered comb. She left the rest hanging in a smooth curtain down my back. My mind ran in circles the whole time, plagued with questions: Why was I suddenly being treated like a lady? How many others had been hired to do my work? What had spurned this sudden change? With a great deal of effort, I held myself still through all of Penelope's meticulous ministrations. Only when she smoothed the last errant lock of hair into place and said, "There you are, my lady, and don't you look a picture?"

did I allow myself to thank her and hurry from the room, intent on interrogating Jack or Philip, whomever I could find first.

I nearly barreled into the buxom maid humming cheerily outside my door. She barely had time to curtsy and wish me good day before I rushed down the stairs. Passing an alarming number of servants along the way, I wondered if Jack and Philip had kept them in reserve for special occasions. In addition to Penelope, I met footmen, housemaids, and even an over-starched butler with too high an opinion of himself.

Pushing my way through the kitchen—peopled with far too many cooks, assistant cooks, and scullery maids—I emerged in the yard. I hated to admit how rattled I was by the number of individuals who had materialized overnight, but I had become accustomed to our quiet lifestyle and the hustle and bustle was disconcerting. Leaning back on the house's gray stone wall for a moment to catch my breath and gather my thoughts, I pulled myself together and made for the stable, checking the garden first for Philip's form. The garden plot, small as it was, boasted three or four individuals tending to the plants, but none of them was Philip. I readjusted my course for the stable, and as I drew nearer I could hear the sounds of men at work, currying horses and cleaning out stalls.

"Be careful with that!" one voice called, louder than the rest. "It may not be the most up-to-date building, but it has done very well for the last seventy years!"

Relief rushed over me as I recognized Jack's voice. Peering over the door, I saw him, hands on hips, getting after a rather young groom who had overenergetically banged a stall door while cleaning. With surprise, I noted Jack's clothing: shiny brown boots instead of work-worn ones, and finely tailored shirt and pants replacing the courser garments he usually donned. *Master Jack indeed.* He seemed to sense my presence and turned around, his face shifting from a stern frown to a welcoming grin. "Bella!" he exclaimed, obviously pleased to see me. "I trust you slept well?"

"And awoke to an entirely different world, it seems," I replied dryly.

He chuckled. "Quite a change, isn't it?" He glanced back to the young man cautiously sweeping out the stall and called out, "That's more like it, Ronald. Keep it up. I want this all clean by midday." He turned back to me. "Shall we take a walk? I can see you're bursting with questions." He stepped out of the stable and offered me his arm, adding in an undertone, "If I have to supervise one more inept groom, someone will get bodily tossed off the property."

I stifled a snigger as I slipped my arm through his. We moved away from the house and stable, the hubbub of workers fading until only the sound of birdsong and breezes filtering through leaves could be heard.

"Now, what would you like to know, Bella?"

I wanted to savor the moment, the appearance of this new Jack who was willing to tell me anything I wished to know. But my curiosity was far too great to be quelled. "Where in the world did all these people come from? And why are they here?"

Motioning me to a fallen tree trunk overshadowed by

rustling branches, he sat beside me. "It was Philip's idea. After you spoke to him yesterday, he couldn't seem to get it out of his head how improper it was for you to be here with only the two of us." I remembered yesterday's conversation about Rose, Jack, and Philip being alone in the household and the troubled expression that had come over Philip's face.

"After discussing it at length, he sent me into town to hire some locals to serve in the house. It's amazing how quickly you can put together an entire household staff when money isn't an issue."

"Money wasn't an issue?" I felt like a parrot repeating what he'd said, but I had never seen evidence of the monetary resources needed for a staff this size.

Jack cast me a knowing glance. "I know what you're thinking. This was practically a hovel when you arrived."

"I wouldn't say that," I lied. "Rundown and unkempt is a better description."

Jack shrugged. "Philip stopped caring about the house and grounds. It was never a matter of funds. The inheritance from his father was quite substantial."

"Apparently it was." I thought of the houseful of servants and staff. "So, since yesterday you hired an entire staff and bought new clothing for all of us?"

"More or less," he replied.

Sensing it was a situation where *more* applied instead of *less*, I asked, "And what about me? Suddenly I'm out of a job and expected to act like a princess?"

He chuckled, the corners of his eyes crinkling. "I told him you wouldn't take kindly to being uprooted, but he would have none of it." Shaking his head, he added, "If it was up to me, you'd have been making bread as usual this morning."

I nudged him with my elbow, unsure if it was just my bread that he missed.

"It's true!" he professed, spreading his hands before him. "I prefer things as they were." The note of defensiveness in his voice caught at me.

"I agree with you," I said. After a moment's hesitation, I added, "But there is something to be said for being treated like a lady for once."

His defensive posture softened. "I would never deprive you of that, Bella."

"You just miss my fresh bread?" I teased.

"Something like that," he replied, dropping his gaze to the ground as if afflicted with bashfulness. I wasn't sure what to make of it. Maybe, like me, he was discomfited at being deprived of his regular occupation.

"And where is the master of the house now?" I asked, with more than a hint of mockery.

"Gone into town again, presumably to acquire something else to improve our lives," he replied, rolling his eyes.

"It can't be all bad," I said. "At least you don't have to muck out the stables by yourself today."

The day passed with agonizing slowness. I hadn't realized how employment made the hours fly by until I was no longer cooking and cleaning every minute of the day. I had been hustled from the kitchen when I tried to lend a helping hand, and I hadn't been allowed to do so much as beat a rug or polish a candlestick anywhere else, so I found myself unaccountably bored. Fancy handwork couldn't hold my attention, and trying to read was out of the question—my mind refused to focus on the page. Jack, my only source of company, had been whisked from my side to oversee the work on the grounds, and Philip had not yet returned from the village. This wasn't surprising, since it was some distance away, but his prolonged absence made me nervous. Some part of me longed to see him striding across the grounds, but another hoped he'd stay away as long as possible.

I racked my brain to remember the particulars of our conversation from the day before: his history, the role Rose had played as his friend and sweetheart, and her sudden disappearance. I reviewed every detail, trying to determine what would drive him to change his household overnight. True, I had commented on the singularity of the situation with Rose, but I had never insinuated—intentionally, at least—that our circumstances were similar. After all, he had loved her. It had been important for everything to be aboveboard and proper. I, on the other hand, had come here as his servant. Philip could never feel the same way about me.

As the day dragged on, I both longed for and dreaded the moment when he would return and offer an explanation for his actions.

"It's time to dress for dinner, my lady," Penelope said, appearing before me in the library.

I looked down at the yellow dress. It had been barely creased by the day's occupations, but I knew better than to expose my humble upbringing by mentioning it. Even a carpenter's daughter knew that fine ladies dressed for supper. Furthermore, this was a day dress, not at all suitable for the occasion. I thought of our casual meals, with the Beast grumbling at the head of the table, and Jack, across from me, making wry observations in order to elicit a laugh or two. It hadn't mattered what I wore then. Now, with everything changing, I felt like I was losing something precious.

Penelope led me to my room, where a beautiful plum-colored gown, edged at neck and sleeves with delicate ivory lace, lay across the bed. Long cream-colored gloves and dainty beaded slippers of the same plum shade sat beside it. "Beautiful," I whispered, fingering the fine fabric. I wondered, not for the first time, how Philip had brought this about so quickly. The house had been woefully neglected, nearly deserted, and thoroughly outdated when I had arrived. Now the place seemed alive, thriving with a full staff and, I had learned, had plans for a full-scale renovation.

"Shall I help you into it, my lady?" Penelope asked politely.

"Yes, please," I replied, turning to allow her to unbutton the day dress.

Anticipation bubbled inside me. The urge to gallop down the stairs was nearly unquenchable. Preceded as I was by the young footman who had summoned me, I reined myself in, remembering to act like a lady. Doing my best to glide down the stairs, I reflected on how the gown fit perfectly—it hugged my figure, highlighting the slimness of my waist and setting off the deep red of the jewel at my throat. My favorite part of the ensemble was the pair of slippers peeping out below the skirt when I stepped forward, their beading catching the light. I had never been dressed so fine.

With a twinge of conscience, I remembered Rose, dressed in the gold gown, bursting with excitement as she hurried down this same staircase. Quickly, I brushed the memory aside, unwilling to let it detract from my own experience.

The footman, a pace or two in front of me, reached the dining room and swung the double doors wide, bowing me past. The room was almost unrecognizable. The walls flickered with candlelight. The small chandelier, which had not been lit in recent history, cast a soft glow over the room. The table and chairs, which had seemed dilapidated yesterday, gleamed like they were new. Elegant dinnerware, shimmering in the soft light, rested on an embroidered ivory tablecloth. The grandness of the room was eclipsed only by the elegance of its occupants.

The gentlemen stood as I entered, greeting me with smiles. Jack, attractive in charcoal trousers and a matching dinner jacket, beamed at me. He was second only to Philip, who for once looked the part of the prosperous landowner in a perfectly fitted black jacket and breeches, shiny knee boots, and a fine-looking shirt topped with a snowy cravat. He smiled shyly at me. Could this be the same being who had treated me so roughly when I first arrived? And had I actually come to value him as a friend? It didn't seem possible, but as I met his serious gray gaze, I knew it was so.

From the head of the table, Philip waved me to the seat on his right, holding the chair until I sat down. Jack grinned at me from across the table as he, too, took his seat. A servant carrying a steaming dish appeared at my elbow, and the meal commenced. Dinner conversation was minimal, focused primarily on the alterations being made to the household. Philip explained that he and Jack had hired a complete staff to care for the house and gardens, and that a full renovation was indeed in the works. New furniture, draperies, and tapestries, as well as bedroom furnishings and linens, would soon be ordered.

My heart sank as I pictured more and more of the world I had become accustomed to vanishing before me. "Is all of this necessary?" I asked, interrupting a discussion between Jack and Philip about overhauling the grounds.

Surprise crossed Philip's face. "Of course it is, Bella. I would have imagined you'd be pleased."

"It isn't that," I chose my words carefully. While I had been sure of myself with the Beast, I didn't know where I stood with Philip, and I didn't want to risk offending him. "I can see the sense of making repairs. But an entire renovation? I'm not certain it's needed."

Beside him, Jack was silent, his eyes glued to his plate. From the expression on his face, I could tell he was listening keenly for Philip's answer. Philip leaned back in his chair to look me over. The way his eyes ran over me reminded me poignantly of the Beast—so calculating it left me feeling exposed. "It's been a long time coming, Bella. Surely you can see that."

I considered for a moment. Wealthy households were always planning remodels and décor updates; it was completely normal. In my long-ago daydreams, I had reveled in the thought of setting those plans into action. More recently, I had imagined remaking this place as it once was. That was all Philip was proposing. So why did it bother me? Dropping my eyes to the linen napkin in my lap, I alternately twisted and smoothed it out while gathering my thoughts.

Jack cleared his throat, and I glanced up to see him stand and push in his chair. "If you'll excuse me, I'll check on the dessert." A look—the type that speaks volumes—passed between the two men before Jack strode to the kitchen.

His expression softening, Philip turned to me as the door closed behind Jack. "What is this about, Bella?"

Those sober gray eyes seemed to draw the truth from me, whether I was ready to face it or not. "Everything is different. Why must all of it change suddenly? I liked it as it was." My voice sounded small. I wasn't used to seeing things spin out of my control. It left me feeling helpless as a child.

"Even the leaky ceiling?" he teased. But I refused to be baited.

He leaned forward, placing a large hand over mine where it fidgeted in my lap. "Please, Bella. Let me do this," he pleaded.

A whuff of a laugh escaped my lips. "This is your home! You can do whatever you like, Philip," I said, not meeting his eye.

"That's not what I meant." Something in his tone made me look up, catching the seriousness in his gaze again. "Let me do this," he reiterated, "for you."

My heart hammered against my ribs, making breathing difficult and speaking even more so.

"I've made mistakes," he went on. "I let the past overshadow my life. You helped me see the error of my ways and brought me back. This is the life you ought to have, Bella. Will you deprive me of providing it for you?"

I swallowed, unsure how to respond. He was offering me everything I'd ever dreamed of. I wondered fleetingly if Jack was listening, and if so, what he would make of the conversation. Thinking of Jack lent me strength, as if even from the other room his influence could reach and calm me. "It's a lovely sentiment, Philip. But I'm not sure I deserve it."

"Of course you deserve it, Bella," he replied, sincerity gleaming in his eyes. "You deserve all of it and more." Gallantly, he lifted my hand and pressed it to his lips. My stomach fluttered as he did so.

"And don't worry about things changing." He smiled up at me. "They can only get better."

I allowed myself to bask in the warmth of his smile for a moment, wanting more than anything to believe his words. As if on cue, lilting music sounded in an adjacent room. Even dazed as I was from our discussion, I couldn't help but recognize the high sweet strain of a violin, with other instruments twining around its lilting melody. Philip stood, resplendent in his dinner attire, and offered me his hand. "Will you honor me with a dance, Bella?"

I tentatively slid my fingers into his, my heart redoubling its hammering as he led me into the parlor, where a quartet had set up. The newly cleaned furniture was pushed to the walls, and the lamplight burned low. In an instant, the past and present merged. Images of Rose and Philip dancing together and the feelings of utter bliss she had experienced superimposed themselves over the moment, filling me with equal amounts of happiness and melancholy. I wanted nothing more than to banish all thoughts of the past, focus only on the present, and melt into Philip. The emotions coursing through me—whether Rose's or mine, I could no longer tell—called for me to surrender myself to him. I struggled to remind myself that I hardly knew this man—as Philip, anyway—no matter what connection to him seemed to pull at my heart.

Oblivious to my mental warfare, Philip took me in his arms and began to spin me around the floor, his grace and training evident. Masterfully, he led me through the steps. The enchantment created by the music, my sur-roundings, and Philip's presence broke down the last of my defenses, and I lost myself to the magic of the moment.

It took me a long time to think of Jack, who had never reappeared from checking on the dessert. Dressed as he had been, surely he'd meant to join us for dancing. With a small grin at the thought of him sauntering across the room to whisk me out of Philip's arms, I glanced about the room to seek him out. At last I saw him, his form no more than a gray smudge in the darkened doorway. A stray beam of light caught his face, and for a moment I thought I saw a stormy look cross his brow. Then Philip spun me around, and when I looked again, the doorway was empty.

Twelve

For you. The words echoed in my mind, murdering hours of sleep. The sudden appearance of the servants, the planned alterations to the house, the strange formality that had crept into our simple lives—it was all done in my behalf. Remembering the feel of Philip's arms around me, so familiar and yet so new at the same time, I yearned for it to be real. All I had ever dreamed of would be mine if it was real, whether or not I was worthy of it. In the days of unloading chores on my siblings and coaxing expensive trinkets out of my father, I had possessed a healthy sense of entitlement. I was certain I would marry well and acquire a comfortable home replete with every luxury. It was only now, after my life had been turned upside down, that I began to doubt myself. Had I done anything to merit all of this? With a man as handsome and charming as Philip offering it to me, I longed for the possibility. I would offer him my heart if it was true.

While pondering this, a vision of Jack poised in the shadows chased away the argument. My feelings for Jack, as difficult to grasp as shadows themselves, could not be disregarded. A fervent friendship had developed between us, and perhaps something more. I chastised myself for even entertaining such a notion when I had just been planning to give my love to Philip. My heart dropped when I thought of the expression on Jack's face before he had disappeared—an indelible, solitary sadness. Is that the expression Philip had received when Rose had chosen him instead of Jack?

Why can't life be simple? I thought, burying my head beneath my pillow in frustration. It had been relatively uncomplicated a few days ago when my only aim had been bettering life for Philip and Jack. Now, with two men before me whom I cared for deeply, everything had become muddled. Groaning, I wrapped the blankets around me, squeezed my eyes tightly shut, and prayed for sleep's oblivion to erase the endless questions from my mind.

His voice was low, intent. "Are you certain?" he asked, his dark eyes serious. I loved those eyes—they were warm and true, as always.

"I love him, Jack. I always have."

Looking away, he scuffed the toe of a work-scarred boot in the dirt. This was not like Jack—the nerves, the seriousness, the absence of his innate optimism. "Do you love him enough to devote yourself entirely to him? To give up your dreams for a life with him?"

Without hesitation, I turned the question back to him. "Dreams? What good are dreams without someone to share them with?"

The concern etched in his eyes didn't diminish. "You know I would never ask you to sacrifice anything for me." A certain intensity I had never heard before flavored his tone and burned in his eyes. "I would do all in my power to see your dreams fulfilled."

My heart softened. I had always loved Jack—his kindness, his bravery, his never-failing friendship—and I would always love him. But it would never be enough. Placing a hand on his cheek, his trim beard tickling my palm, I said softly, "I could never ask it of you, Jack. I love Philip."

He pulled away, his eyes bright with unshed tears. "You don't believe I could provide a life for you—make your aspirations a reality." He looked away. "You don't think I'm worthy of you."

"No!" I said fiercely, my heart breaking at the pain I had inflicted. Clutching handfuls of his rough shirt in my hands, I buried my face in his chest. Tears rolled down my cheeks. His smell and the feel of his body against mine were so familiar; I had come here in search of solace, counsel, and comfort countless times. Unlike before, this time his arms hung woodenly at his sides. Shaken, I babbled on, trying to repair the rift I had created. "Never say that, Jack. You are my best friend. I can't live without you. I'm the one who's unworthy of you and all you would sacrifice for me."

He gently eased the fabric out of my hands and stepped away. His shirt front was damp with my tears. "I'm sorry, Rose. I never should have spoken." He swiped a hand over his eyes, turned, and walked away.

Answering tears flowed down my cheeks as I awoke, still wrapped in the fringes of the dream. The room was dark, my window showcasing an array of stars pinpricking the black sky. Visions of Jack layered over one another, recent events mingling with those of the past. The hurt expression from the previous night was only a twinge compared to how his face had crumbled when Rose had unwittingly broken his heart. Then, he'd worn the hopeless look of a man on the rack whose torturers had given the lever its final twist. If I had been Rose, facing him afterward would have been unbearable.

Lying there in my bed, waiting for my emotions to subside, I reflected—with dissatisfaction—how they were beginning to mirror Rose's feelings toward both Jack and Phillip. It had not been my intention to pick up the reins where she had dropped them. That was as good as trailing behind a runaway steed headed toward tragedy. My desire had been to clean up the mess she had made, not add to it in a way that would damage one, if not both, of the men I had come to admire.

I couldn't live with that outcome.

Was that why Rose left? Had she been unable to accept the fact that in choosing Philip, she had wounded Jack? Did the daily reminder of her choice become too difficult to bear, or had something else come into play? I decided to speak with Jack as soon as possible and undo whatever damage had already been done. Face to face, I could assure him of the depth of my regard for him and do whatever was necessary to safeguard our friendship.

Without his unwavering kindness and support, I didn't think I could carry on. He was my ballast, my anchor in this strange new life. Without him, I would drift dangerously. Pulling my resolve around me, I told myself that I would be successful where Rose had failed.

I had to be.

My plan to set things right with Jack was thwarted as soon as I opened my eyes. I had vowed to arise early and meet him before he attended to his duties, but a night riddled with disconcerting dreams had left me too groggy to arise at even my regular hour. I awakened at last to the smell of hot breakfast—blessedly, *not* porridge.

"Breakfast, my lady?"

Resigned to the fact that I'd missed my chance to speak privately with Jack and would have to find another occasion, I cracked open an eye to see Penelope standing beside my bed. She placed a breakfast tray on my lap as I sat up. I snatched up a slice of bacon but refrained from shoving it into my mouth, instead nibbling it while scooping up a forkful of eggs with the other hand. The erratic emotions of the night had left me ravenous.

Penelope rooted about in my closet, emerging a short time later with a beautifully tailored deep green riding habit. *Where had that come from?* I wondered. If there hadn't been another piece of bacon at hand, nothing could have stopped me from conducting a full exploration of the closet to discover its secrets.

"Master Philip requests you ride out with him this morning, my lady. When you've finished with your meal, of course," Penelope said, narrowly eyeing the bacon dangling from my fingertips. It was as close as she had come to disapproval in the twenty-four hours I had known her. I placed the bacon back on the plate, somewhat chagrined. Carpenters' daughters, who might be less knowledgeable about other rules of etiquette, knew they shouldn't eat with their hands, even if it was deliciously crisp bacon. *Acting the part of a lady can be quite tedious*, I reflected as I finished by meal. Then, swinging my legs out of bed, I resigned myself to Penelope's ministrations, however tiresome they might be.

A short time later, I found myself dressed in the green riding habit and brown boots laced to the knee. My hair had been brushed for longer than I could patiently bear—until it literally gleamed—and Penelope had swept it up and pinned a clever little hat on top.

Hurrying downstairs, I hoped to catch Jack before departing, but once again fate was not on my side. The overstarched butler ushered me outside, where Philip was waiting, his horse saddled and pawing at the ground. A groom held my readied mount beside him. Philip looked me up and down approvingly as he boosted me into the saddle. "You look lovely, Bella."

I felt my cheeks burn at the compliment and smiled uncertainly down at him. He was as tall as ever, but he looked less imposing without his shaggy hair, his wild beard, and his perpetual scowl. I pulled myself together enough to respond, "Thank you, Philip. You're looking quite well this morning too."

He had the decency to look abashed as he swung into the saddle, but he was undoubtedly aware of his own good looks. In my days of attending balls, dinner parties, and afternoon soirées with the purpose of attaching myself to a wealthy—and if at all possible, handsome—young gentleman, I had never met his equal. I watched him out of the corner of my eye as we set out at a slow trot, noting the thick black hair hanging carelessly on his brow, his long, expressive face, and his soulful eyes. He struck me, like he always had in my dreams, as extremely attractive, but there was something new in his posture today. Where the Beast had skulked, every movement broadcasting his certainty of the world's disapproval, Philip strode out confidently, head held high. It was as if he was a different person altogether. I wasn't sure what to make of him—or the tender feelings for him that were beginning to flower within me.

Knowingly, he flicked his gaze to me. "Something on your mind, Bella?"

Unwilling to give him any hint of my present train of thought, I pretended I hadn't heard, refocusing my eyes on the path before me.

"I know that look well," he said wryly. "It means you have something to say but will keep me in the dark until I bully it out of you."

"Surely *you* have never bullied me into anything, Philip," I retorted archly.

I was gratified with low chuckle. "Touché," he conceded. His expression sobered as he continued, "Though I will have to atone for all my past transgressions, no matter the circumstances under which they were committed." He let this sink in for a moment before adding, "That's part of the reason I invited you out today, Bella—to begin to make up for my past behavior." His eyes lingered on me, gauging my reaction. "I was also hoping for a chance to get to know you better."

"Don't you already know me?" I asked. From the beginning, he had professed to know everything about me, and, irritatingly, his assumptions had been quite accurate.

"I feel there is more to know," he replied. "When roses bloom, they reveal their beauty petal by petal."

The elegance of his remark was marred by the reference to roses. It was certainly not intended to remind me of his past love, but it did so just the same. He had known her perfectly, or thought he had, and she had known him. Could I ever hope to understand him as she had?

As if reading my thoughts, he asked quietly, "Do you know me, Bella?"

Do I know him? I thought I had come to understand the Beast fairly well, with his gruff ways and strange insights. My perceptions of Philip as part of Rosalind's life had been relatively clear also. But the man before me, a hybrid of both, was an enigma. How much of him was Rose's Philip, and how much was the Beast?

"What you are too polite to say is that you don't know me," he stated when I didn't respond. "Which is something of a relief, actually, since the man you knew wasn't much of a man to begin with." His brows drew down in consternation. Was he remembering the personage he had been, whose appearance was nearly as off-putting as his personality? I studied him for a moment and wondered where that abrasive personality had gone. Was it a part of him still?

At last, he looked up. "Here is what I propose: we take time to come to know one another properly. Start afresh."

I nodded slowly. It seemed sensible enough. "I believe we have both changed a great deal lately. I hardly know myself," I admitted. "I would welcome a chance to come to know you better, Philip."

He treated me to a smile that reached all the way to his eyes. "Then let's get started," he said, gripping his reins a little tighter. "The first thing you should know about me is that I don't like to lose!" With that, he dug in his heels, his mount springing into action.

And the first thing you should know about me, I thought, digging in my own heels and leaning forward to push the horse into a gallop, *is that I* never *lose.*

We settled into our places in the study that evening, I in my easy chair by the fire, Philip beside me in his own. Although it wasn't exactly playing out as our previous evenings had, at least the scene was familiar. No longer allowed to attend to the mending, I kept my hands busy with embroidery. And Philip, instead of sitting in an armchair situated as far away as possible while still being in the same room, sat beside me and made a concerted effort to find books on subjects that captured my interest rather than selecting thick, dust-covered volumes about breeding new species of who knew what.

My needle flew as he read epic tales of heroism, bravery, and romance. They reminded me of evenings at home, the room quiet but for Father's low, smooth voice, Cassie's clicking needles, and the soft scraping of Aaron's knife as he whittled. I would curl up in the window seat, weaving daydreams, tracking the flickering flames in the hearth, or gazing out at the star-littered sky while my thoughts would dwell on illustrious balls, rich carriages, and handsome noblemen. Those simpler days seemed unbelievably far away now—part of another girl's life.

Philip's deep tone, much less gruff than it had once been, intruded on my reverie. When he read aloud, his voice took on a sonorous quality, but now, it was bent in a question. "Are you all right, Bella?" He closed the book, careful to mark his place, and turned to me. "Something bothering you?"

A bittersweet feeling tugged at me. "I was thinking of my family."

"Really?" he said. "You've never told me about them."

I thought for a moment before speaking. "There were just the four of us—my father; my sister, Cassie; my brother, Aaron; and myself."

"And your mother?"

"She died when I was young. Cassie is the only one who remembers her well." To me, my mother had become little more than a distant, though pleasant, memory. Other than the small portrait my father treasured, I didn't recall what she looked like, though I knew Cassie, with her fair hair and golden beauty, took after her.

"You miss her?"

"A little. I think what I miss most is the *idea* of having a mother," I replied.

His brows rumpled together as if he was trying to make sense of what I'd said. "What do you mean?"

"A mother might have been able to curb my behavior and lead me in the right direction. My father hadn't a prayer. I could bend him to my will from infancy."

Philip's low chuckle sounded. "So the strong-willed act wasn't for my benefit?"

"Oh, no," I assured him with a shake of my head and a tiny smirk. "I have always been able to get the upper hand."

He chuckled again. "What about your older sister?"

"Cassie is perfectly lovely, kind, and gifted at everything she puts her hand to. She tried to lend a hand in my upbringing, but her nature is too soft," I replied. "In fact, everything about her is angelic. No doubt you would find her more attractive than me."

He should have contradicted me. Wasn't that the way men were supposed to respond when a woman acknowledged another as her superior in beauty or accomplishments? But no such gallant contradiction was forthcoming.

"She sounds . . . perfect." Something gleamed deep in his eyes and echoed in his pause. Perhaps a glimmer of interest in Cassie? The fact that I was used to it made it nonetheless irritating. Perhaps sensing his mistake, he changed the subject.

"And your brother?"

Eager to avoid dwelling on Cassie's endless virtues, I addressed the question quickly. "Aaron is young and brilliant, but he's too engrossed in his inventions to care overmuch about anything else. He's my genius younger brother." I paused before adding, "Unfortunately, I discovered his temper too late—after I had pushed him past his limit."

Philip's eyebrows rose in silent inquiry, and without further ado, I recounted the events that had led me to his doorstep: my indolence and obsession with pretty things, my father's illness, and Cassie and Aaron's growing frustration with me. All I had accomplished in Philip's household as opposed to all my brother and sister had done at home while I had shirked responsibility made me feel twitchy in my own skin. I didn't like to think about it.

Philip cleared his throat. "I can't imagine you as such a non-industrious character, Bella. I had to employ a household of servants to accomplish what you did on your own."

My lips curved up into half a smile. "I wasn't the same girl then, and if I hadn't been thrown into service as your maid, I might never have changed."

Philip accepted this without comment, so I continued with the tale, relating the gifts that father had brought for us.

"Aren't you leaving something out?" Philip interrupted, his keen eyes fixed on me.

As gently as possible, I said, "What would you like me to say? You know better than anyone what happened to my father."

He watched me for a moment, his eyes hard as flint one moment and soft as a cloud the next. "Very well," he said at last. "What gift did he bring for you?"

I flicked my gaze up to his, sure he had already guessed. "This," I said, lifting the jewel where it hung around my neck. The misery I had tried to save him scrolled across his face.

"It wasn't your fault," I rushed to reassure him.

"How so?" he inquired, a small amount of the old bitterness lacing his tone. "Did someone else imprison your father for finding it in the forest? You said it yourself—no one knows better than I what happened. I'm fully aware of what I did, Bella."

"That may be so, but no one knows better than I how you have changed." I steadied my emotions before continuing. "And it was I who asked him for it. It was my greed that led him to seek it out." It was the first time I had owned this fact aloud.

"Come now, Bella. We know who is to blame."

I leaned forward slightly to meet his gaze fully. "If you could have seen me, completely oblivious to my father's presence—though he had been gone for months—you would understand," I said. "He had already told us what the jewel had cost him, but nothing could keep me from wearing it. The rest of the day, instead of thinking of the man who had sacrificed so much to give it to me, I could only think of how others would admire it at the next ball."

Philip shook his head. "That only betrays a preference for pretty things, like most girls. Nothing more serious than that, Bella."

"Perhaps," I conceded. "But the conclusion I have come to is that everything that happened afterward was spurned by my actions, and most assuredly by my disregard for my family."

He considered this for a moment, propping an elbow on the arm of his chair and cupping his cheek with one hand.

"And my siblings agreed."

"How do you know?"

"In the morning, they sent me away." I didn't want to relate that midnight conversation. The realization that I was to blame for much of what happened hadn't dulled my humiliation.

"No wonder," Philip commented, his long fingers tented under his chin and his expression contemplative.

"No wonder?" I repeated.

"No wonder you fought me like a wild animal when I found you. You had just lost everything." He turned his gaze to the dancing flames in the hearth. "It grieves me that my actions caused you to lose everything you knew and loved, Bella." His tone was edged with sorrow.

"It was my own doing," I replied softly. "The first time I realized I had something to lose was when I had already lost it. Before then, I prayed for freedom from my mundane life. Until I was cut free, I didn't understand how wonderful that life was." Putting those sentiments into words felt strange, and saying them made me feel better and worse at the same time. I remembered the numbness I had experienced after my siblings had sent me away, the freedom I'd prayed for bringing with it an unanticipated sense of loneliness. I'd had little time to consider how utterly lost I had felt before fate had intervened and landed me at Philip's feet.

"Then you came here." His brow furrowed as he picked up the thread of the tale. "And your reception was less than cordial."

A small smile pulled at my lips. "I do remember you providing me with prime accommodations and wholesome gruel that first evening."

He chuckled mirthlessly. "Even exhausted and with your pride wounded, you would have none of it. The pampered princess . . ."

The smile spreading over my face turned sardonic. "Only the best for Bella."

"Like the first meal you served us?" he needled, one corner of his mouth quirking up.

"High class cuisine," I pronounced. In an undertone, I added, "Though I may have mixed up the soup with the wash water that first day."

His laughter rang through the room, full and genuine. When it faded away, a sober expression painted his features. "Not that I didn't deserve it, after the way I treated your father. And you."

"For my part, it was nothing my conduct didn't merit." With a pang, I remembered the numerous things Jack had done to make the situation more bearable, and added, "And at least Jack was always kind."

"Yes," he agreed. "That's his way. He has always been a far better friend than I deserved."

Mentioning Jack made me glance around the room, as if I might find him hiding in a shadowy corner, listening to every word of our conversation. But the corners were empty.

Since dinner last night, Jack had faded into the background. Without his warm, comforting presence and his friendship and camaraderie, the house felt emptier even though it was now filled with people. *I must find a time to speak with him soon*, I thought.

"What would you do if you could see your family again?" Philip asked, drawing my thoughts away from Jack.

Tucking my needle into the fabric, I set my embroidery in my lap. "I promised myself that when I see them again I will do my best to make amends, doing whatever is necessary to correct the past."

He looked me over approvingly, his lips curving into a small smile.

Finding an opportunity for a private tête-à-tête with Jack was proving more difficult than I anticipated. It seemed that whenever I wanted to seek him out, Penelope would appear with a summons from Philip. At first, I was somewhat wary of all the attention Philip showered on me, although not so long ago I would have reveled in the attentions of a wealthy and attractive prospect like him. But then, I found the picnics, afternoon rides, private breakfasts, and comfortable conversations in the library enjoyable. I kept expecting him to act like the Beast, but he was always good-humored, though sober, as was his nature.

Our activities filled most of the day, and the only time I saw Jack was at dinner, when others were present and private conversation was impossible. Everything about Jack's demeanor, which was perfectly polite, indicated that he didn't hold any ill will toward me. All the same, I sensed something was amiss and feared I had done something grave to make him keep his distance in such a fashion. Besides dinner, on the rare occasion when I did have a free moment, I could never seem to find Jack. It was as if he was pointedly avoiding me, as I had once done to him.

Unable to stand it any longer, I feigned illness one night, intent on cornering him and getting to the truth of the matter. Penelope hovered nervously over me, clucking like a mother hen, until I convinced her that I was retiring for the night and preferred to do so in solitude. Waiting for her footsteps to fade down the hall, I slipped my dressing gown back on and stood beside the door. Jack's familiar tread sounded on the stair, pausing as he reached my room. An almost imperceptible sigh escaped him as he stood there. The shadow blocking the band of light under the door seemed to waver before it passed on. After his door clicked shut, I listened to make sure Philip was safely ensconced in his study. As long as he was engrossed in one of his dusty tomes, he would be insensible to anything else. Cautiously, I crept down the hall to Jack's door. My days as housemaid had taught me it was never locked, so without knocking, I swung it open, stepped inside, and shut it behind me.

Sitting on the edge of the bed, Jack looked up, astonishment written in every feature. He had begun to undress for the night. His shirt was untucked and open at the collar. The sight of his bare throat caught me off guard, and I couldn't help but notice the way the muscles corded along his collarbones. Idly, I remembered wrapping my arms around him as we had ridden together and feeling his work-hardened abdomen under my hands. These recollections, along with the sudden realization that I had entered unbidden into his bedchamber in little more than my nightgown, brought home the inappropriateness of the situation. After spending every spare second thinking about Jack and what I would say when given the chance, now that the moment was here, I was without words.

"Bella," he said, when the silence stretched on, "what are you doing here?"

I swallowed, gathering my wits and avoiding looking directly at him. "I've been meaning to talk to you, Jack."

"In my room? At this hour?"

I held my ground and continued to meet his eye.

"All right," he said resignedly, motioning toward the plain wooden chair beside his bed, "have a seat."

Nervously, I did as he directed, tucking my hands into my lap to keep myself from fidgeting, and forcing my mind into motion. All the carefully crafted phrases had vanished, leaving only the naked truth. "I've missed spending time with you . . . ," I began, then hesitated. It felt too honest. I wanted to take it back as soon as it had left my lips.

He replied, "So have I. But you've been busy."

I didn't mention the fact that he had been no more available than I. "Philip seems bent on making up for all the times he treated me like a scullery maid."

He huffed out a laugh, and I looked up. His dark eyes were crinkled in amusement at the corners but tinged with sadness in their depths. "He can be quite persistent."

"What I can't determine is what he's doing so persistently."

"Can't you?" he replied quietly, his shoulders stooped and his eyes downcast. Then he seemed to mentally shake himself, squaring his shoulders and meeting my gaze once more. "He's the happiest I've seen him in a long time."

"Really?" Part of me wanted to believe it.

"Yes," he said softly. "I haven't seen him like this since before Rose left."

I don't want to talk about Rose and Philip, I thought, my insides twisting as they always did when I thought of them together. *What* did *I want to talk about?* My mind balked at the question, and instead of facing it, I turned the query back to Jack. "And you?" I asked. "Have you been unhappy since Rose left?"

His eyes flicked to my face, as if the question surprised him. "We were both a little damaged when she left. But hard work is its own sort of comfort, as you well know."

I quirked an eyebrow at him, not understanding what he meant.

"I may have been listening to your conversation in the library," he admitted, somewhat sheepishly.

I remembered thinking of him while I was relating my history to Philip, and I wondered if I had somehow sensed his presence. I offered him a small smile. "And now I am the open book, it seems."

"You were never very good at concealment anyway, Bella." He eyed me for a second. "Manipulation, perhaps, but not concealment."

I conceded the point with a nod. "Speaking of being an open book, there's still something I haven't discovered yet. When Rose left, were you heartbroken like Philip?" I was being unaccountably nosy, I knew, but I had to learn the truth. Jack had never admitted to anything more than friendship with Rose, but I knew his affection for her ran far deeper.

He considered for a moment before answering. "I was sad to lose a friend, but it was Philip she loved. He was the fiancé she left behind. Not me."

It was neither the admission I was fishing for nor the denial I wished to hear. "Did that matter?"

"In the end, no. We suffered just the same."

Except that instead of burying himself in sorrow, Jack had buried his sorrow in work. My heart went out to him. "You loved her," I said finally, needing to see his reaction to the statement. He didn't argue. He just put his head in his hands. "Then why didn't you go after her?"

After a moment of silence, he replied, "Because I was the reason she left."

Thirteen

hat's not possible."

"It's true," he insisted miserably, his head still cradled in his hands, his dejected pose a testament of his guilt. "I told her to follow her dreams, and she did." The details of my latest vision flooded over me—Jack asking Rose if she was certain about her life with Philip and urging her not to give up on her aspirations. Had she deserted them both to fulfill those dreams in the end?

I should have felt more sympathetic, but a well of irritation bubbled up within me. "All the more reason to go after her," I said stubbornly. I was still struggling to understand why neither of them had pursued the woman they claimed to care for so deeply.

"I couldn't," he said, his voice breaking as he raised his face from his hands, his eyes full of anguish and shining with tears. "She left because of me. I couldn't have deserted Philip after that. He wouldn't have survived."

The pieces fell into place at last. This was Jack's true reason for remaining by his friend's side. I stepped from the chair to sit beside him on the bed, wrapping an arm around him and laying my head on his bowed shoulder. "It wasn't your fault," I consoled him. "She made her own decision, regardless of what you may have said or done."

"But I urged her to do it, to doubt her love for him and choose another path," he persisted.

"And you've been living with it all this time," I said gently. Of the two men who had suffered when Rose left, Jack had suffered the most, though he had shown it the least. How I admired him for that. Thinking of the dream of Rose, I mused aloud, "I believe she did love you, Jack, in her own way."

"Maybe," he relented. "But what difference did it make?"

Unsure how to address that question, I nestled against him to comfort him in his grief. If I could not help him unload the burden, at least I could share it. Feeling indelibly connected to him in that moment, the words slipped out before I knew it. "I love you."

What had I just said? Had I really just professed my love for Jack?

The utter, plain truth, my heart answered, thrumming with the revelation. I wanted to hide from it, to take it back as soon as it slipped out.

I felt him stiffen beneath my arm. "That's impossible," he said slowly, straightening and facing me, the pallor in his face deepening, his eyes still, dark pools. "You love Philip. I see it in every look you give him. You're just like her."

I didn't know how to respond. Being compared to Rose only twisted my stomach in more knots. My feelings toward Philip were too new, too undeveloped to fathom. How could I deny the fact that he was everything I'd ever looked for in a man? But my affection for Jack, revealed in that very moment, was nonetheless real.

"I owe him this," he said, shrugging my arm off and rising to his feet to put more space between us. "I won't stand in his way, not this time. I couldn't bear to see him hurt again." He moved to the door, his face resolute, his momentary weakness hidden behind an expressionless mask. Only his eyes, full of torment, gave him away. "It's time for you to go, Bella," he said, his voice devoid of emotion.

Numbly, I watched him open the door, peer out to be sure the corridor was empty, and then stand aside expectantly. I rose from the edge of the bed, feeling a chill so strong it made my bones ache, though the room was the same temperature it had been moments ago. Longing to touch him, I paused in the doorway, pressing my hands to my sides to keep them in check. "Good night, Jack." It was all I could say. I slipped into the darkened hallway.

"Good-bye, Bella," he whispered hoarsely after me.

Before I left Jack's room, I had never understood the feeling of heartbreak. But now my insides felt like they were being torn apart and drowned in a well of hopelessness. This could be nothing else. Lying in the dark, staring up at my bedroom ceiling, the conversation with Jack replayed in my mind. *How could I have been so stupid?* To

speak without thinking, as I was so apt to do, had sev-
ered my bond with someone I cared for deeply. Someone
I loved. The realization that my careless tongue had done
such damage was only slightly less painful than the realization that Jack didn't love me in return. In my mind I
had built up the idea of a person content to worship from
afar as the pinnacle of romantic love. Now I had put my
heart in another's hands and received only anger, frustration, and rejection. My feelings on the matter were quite
the reverse of what they had been.

I squeezed my eyes shut, conjuring up images of home,
of the simple life of daydreams and ambitions. Even as
I pulled them forward, I saw what an empty existence it
had been. I'd had only dreams where love played no part,
a life where I bartered, manipulated, and frittered away
all the familial love I possessed in pursuit of *things*. Was
this to be my fate, living unloved and alone because of
the choices I had made?

Unbidden, Philip's face came to mind: kind and sensitive, his eyes lighting up when I stepped into the room,
his attention focused solely on me. The inner ache eased
as I thought of him. *Did I love him?* The feelings were
still too fresh to fathom, but I hadn't known my feelings
for Jack, either, until they had tumbled off my tongue.

Jack. My heart hurt, and I banished all thought of
him. If he truly did not love me, there was nothing I
could do to change his mind. But Philip—I had a chance
for a good life with him, and I could not cast that aside
because I had been ridiculous enough to throw myself
at another. I rolled onto my side, curled into a ball, and
tucked the blankets tightly under my chin. Fishing for

happier memories, I recalled the night when I had spun in Philip's arms. I tried to recapture his scent, the feel of his arms around me, and the expression of joy that had burned in his eyes. But even in the middle of that perfect scene, my mind turned to the shadowy form poised in the doorway, threatening to mar our happiness.

Bright morning beams streaming through the windows at the end of the hallway caught Philip in a wide band of light. "Bella, how are you feeling today?" he asked, a look of concern on his face.

I grimaced, knowing that no amount of expensive clothing and careful hairstyling could disguise another restless night. "I'm fine," I assured him.

"Perhaps you just need some fresh air," he suggested. "I can have the cook ready a picnic for this afternoon."

With a headache threatening at my temples, the last thing I wanted to do was ride out in full daylight with wind snatching at my clothing. But after my conversation with Jack, I had decided to do my best to forget him and encourage Philip's attentions—allowing the feelings I had for Philip a chance to come to fruition in the process. Forcing my lips into a smile, I replied in what I hoped was a genial tone, "That sounds perfect, Philip."

The wide grin that spread over his face was reward enough for my efforts. And, I thought, surely Penelope could produce a sun hat from my abundant collection to shield my eyes from the bright afternoon rays.

The day was overcast, which saved me from developing a full-blown headache, though my temples throbbed dully under the wide-brimmed hat Penelope had provided. Each breath of fresh air and each smooth stride the horses took away from the house cleared my mind and lightened the weight in my chest. Perhaps Philip was right. Perhaps this was what I needed. Every moment I spent in his presence was like a balm to my soul, uplifting and strengthening. As long as I didn't allow my mind to dwell on Jack and all that had occurred the previous night, I could bear up passably well. I hadn't seen Jack at all, and though part of me wanted to make things right, another part of me was too humiliated to seek another confrontation.

Philip glanced over at me. "You're awfully quiet today."

I curved my lips into a small smile in an attempt to assuage his concern.

True to his nature, he saw past the façade. "Need I mention how uncharacteristic it is for you to keep your thoughts to yourself?"

I weighed my words, reluctant to reveal any portion of the interchange with Jack. "I had a bad night. But you were quite right; the fresh air is making me feel much better."

He arched an eyebrow. "I almost believe you."

I chuckled. He knew me too well. "Trust me when I say that it's nothing you need to be worried about."

"All the same . . . ," he prompted expectantly.

"All the same," I replied, "I'd prefer to spend the afternoon enjoying the beauty of the outdoors instead of wasting it by dwelling on unpleasantness. Wouldn't you?"

He grinned knowingly. "Indeed. But," he added, "I am ready to listen when your tongue loosens."

A genuine smile spread over my lips. "Thank you, Philip."

We picnicked in a secluded grove of trees, surrounded by the soft sounds of birds nesting in the branches and the gurgle of a nearby stream. Philip spread a blanket on the ground and proceeded to unpack edibles from the saddle bags. He started in on his own plate only after he had piled one high and thrust it into my hands.

"Now eat like a good girl," he ordered. "You still look worn out, and I won't have anyone saying I mistreat my guests."

I eyed the plate brimming with juicy grapes, fresh bread, and buttery cheeses, but I had no appetite. I wondered how I would ever make Philip believe I wasn't ill when he found that out. I could never hope to eat half of what he'd given me, but I obediently popped a grape into my mouth.

Hoping to distract him from the fact that I was mostly just moving the food around my plate, I said, "This is a beautiful spot. What made you choose it for our outing?"

He looked up from his lunch and shrugged. "It was one of my father's favorite places. It reminds me of him."

"Why is that?" I pressed, making myself start in on the bread and cheese.

"He always brought my mother here. It was their special place." He motioned toward a nearby tree with a scarred trunk. "See? He carved their initials there when they were courting." I could just make out faint letter-like markings surrounded by a lopsided heart. It was something my father would have done for my mother, and it touched me more than I cared to admit. "After she died," Philip continued soberly, "he brought Jack and me to picnic or hunt through the trees and track animals. I think he felt closer to her here."

I imagined an older version of Philip taking the young boys to his favorite haunt. Maybe the inability to let go of lost love had passed from father to son. I couldn't help asking, "Did you and Rose have a special place?"

With a crease in his brow, he dropped his gaze back to his plate and rolled a grape back and forth. "This was ours too."

I glanced at the trees and noted, a bit farther off, another scarred tree trunk with a rough heart carved into the surface. Something about the sight saddened me, as if my presence intruded on the memory of what had once been.

"I shouldn't have brought you here," he said remorse-fully. "I didn't think."

Pushing aside the feeling of encroaching on the past, I set my plate down and slid over to his side so I could link my fingers with his. I would do my best to forget my feelings for Jack and fully explore the possibility of a union with Philip. "I'm glad you brought me here." At this, he looked over at me, eyebrows raised in puzzle-ment. Leaning my head on his shoulder, I added, "This old place needs some new memories."

The afternoon was spent in quiet conversation. Philip taught me about the plants and animals that inhabited the forest. I had known he was well-informed on many subjects, but he had never been talkative enough to reveal the extent of his knowledge. Curled together on the blanket and tramping hand-in-hand through the woods, he relaxed and revealed more of himself than he had before. The touch of his arm around my waist and his hand in mine drove away the dark thoughts that had riddled my mind during the morning.

Fingers intertwined, we hiked a nearby hill at the close of day, settling on a boulder at the hill's crest to watch the sun retreat behind the faraway mountains. Brilliant scarlet and coral swept across the heavens, fading to pink as the sun dipped lower. Reluctant to leave, we watched the color drain from the sky, the pale blue deepening to slate, all the while wrapped securely in one another's arms.

When we returned to the house, it was quite late. Jack had already eaten his dinner and retired for the evening. My relief tinged with guilt filled me when I didn't have to face him. The day had been so perfect, and I dreaded spoiling it with a renewal of the sentiments from the night before. At the same time, a piece of me longed for Jack's company. But that was lost to me now, I reminded myself. Three fateful words had ensured that nothing between Jack and I would ever be the same.

Philip and I took our meal in the library in order to continue our conversation before the crackling fire. As he teased and talked, I wondered if the hole that had been left by Jack could be filled by Philip. Could I love Philip the way Rosalind had, with an all-consuming passion that would inspire me to abandon my life's ambitions for him? My dilemma wasn't the same as Rosalind's, I realized—instead of abandoning my dreams by linking my life with Philip's, they would be fulfilled. Our courtship—it could be called nothing less—had moved along rapidly. In a matter of months, I had gone from living with my family to serving as Philip's maid and finally to settling into my new place as his cherished guest. I didn't dare call myself anything more, at least until he declared his intentions.

In the flickering firelight, Philip's gray eyes brimmed with affection, and I hoped that he could someday come to feel the same passion for me as he had for Rose.

After spending the days with Philip on picnics, outings, and in pleasant conversations in the library, we dined together in the evenings. Typically, it was similar to the first evening after his return from the village, except Jack was invariably absent. Penelope produced an unlimited number of attractive evening gowns—enough to satisfy even my desires—and the table was furnished with elegant dinnerware and scrumptious dishes. The flickering light cast from tall silver candlesticks lent the room an air of intimacy. Philip took advantage of the ambience to cast any number of smoldering glances, tender gazes, and boyish grins at me. However, his face was unusually sober on one night in particular.

Taking my hand in his, he said, "Bella, we began on a rather rocky foundation, didn't we?"

I couldn't keep a tiny smile from escaping at this understatement. Our first meeting had been a nightmare—his dark form materializing out of the forest to frighten my horse half to death, then looming disapprovingly over me, carrying me roughly, and throwing me into the cellar.

"But spending nearly every day in your company, I have come to care for you. Deeply," Philip continued.

My smile broadened, and I squeezed his hand, thinking of how things had changed since my arrival. We had truly started on shaky ground, and without Jack's intervention—*why can't I keep him out of my thoughts?*—we might have torn each other apart. In time, we had become tolerant of one another, and an uneasy friendship had developed. Finally, that respect had evolved into a genuine relationship. After I had done all in my power to help him, he'd turned the tables on me, transforming from something beastly into the perfect gentleman.

Now here he was, his eyes grave, his fingers holding mine tightly.

"Will you do me the honor of marrying me?"

My breath caught in my throat. My mind had been roaming through the past, and now it was jolted back to the present. His eyes, the soft gray of a stormy sky, and the look on his face, a mingling of sincerity and tenderness, warmed my heart. My tongue temporarily bound, I could do no more than gaze into those expressive eyes.

His lips quirked up on one corner, easing the

seriousness of his expression. "It's customary for the lady to give some sort of reply."

"I . . . ," I faltered, unsure of how to proceed. In my girlhood daydreams, I had composed countless flowery speeches in answer to the fateful question. Now that the moment had arrived, they had all deserted me.

"Please, Bella. I can't imagine my life without you," he said, squeezing my hand even tighter. "Say you'll be mine."

My mind lurched, and I could think only of Rose. And Jack. "Are you certain?" I had to ask.

"You brought me back, Bella, and reminded me of who I am. I owe you everything," he declared.

Coldness settled into my stomach at his last words, and I pulled my hand from his. "I do not wish to be married out of a sense of duty. You owe me nothing." I tucked my hands into my lap and dropped my gaze from his. Even in the moment, I realized the singularity of my reaction. In my former life, if a gentleman as handsome and affluent as Philip had asked for my hand, I would have had no qualms in accepting him whether I loved him or not.

Truly, my life had turned upside down.

"Bella," he chided. "You don't actually think . . ." I could feel his keen eyes scrutinizing me, but I refused to look up. I heard him move from his chair to kneel beside mine. He placed a palm under my chin, gently lifting my face until our eyes met. "Don't you know already? I've said it in my head a million times: I love you, Bella."

At that he leaned forward, tipping his face up to meet mine and covering my mouth with his. His scent, that delicious aroma from Rose's memory, was nothing compared to his taste. I drank him in like one who has gone without water for days and is given wine instead. The euphoria left me light-headed. He drew back, looking at me and stroking my cheek with his thumb. "Well?" he asked softly. "What is it to be, my beauty?"

I scoffed, the magic of the moment dissipating at the compliment, so incongruous with the truth. "Beauty?" I said, shaking my head. "You *must* love me if you think me a beauty, Philip."

His eyes narrowed. I recognized that look, which warned of danger on the horizon. Quickly I amended my statement. "I keep forgetting that you've never met my sister. Compared to her golden-haired perfection, I'm rather ordinary."

His eyes softened, and he took my hands in his. "Not to me." This time it was I who initiated the kiss; the adoration on his face was irresistible. "Bella," he half-groaned against my lips, his nose still brushing mine, "how many times are you going to make me ask you to marry me before you give me a proper answer?"

I chuckled, pulling away slightly to take in the look of half-torture, half-pleasure painted across his features. "At least one more time. I couldn't have you thinking I'm an easy sell."

He had the decency not to roll his eyes, instead allowing only a sigh of frustration to escape. He composed his face into seriousness again. "Bella, will you be my wife?"

I closed the distance between us until only a breath separated us. I brushed his mouth with mine before I whispered "Yes," and once again pressed my lips to his.

Fourteen

A palpable air of excitement drew me from dream-land unnaturally early the next morning. I had little time to wonder at its cause, for as soon as I was awake, Penelope and a gaggle of women from the household—giddy with anticipation for my upcoming nuptials—descended upon me. Armed to the teeth with wedding clothes, brushes, ribbons, and elegant combs, they went into action. It terrified me more than I cared to admit.

Philip works quickly, I couldn't help thinking, admiring the wedding dress, veil, and slippers he had already procured. The white satin gown and beaded slippers were exquisite, and excitement welled up inside me when Penelope helped me into them. The dress's cap sleeves were constructed of pearl beads over filmy fabric, the bodice was plain but fitted, and the full skirt and long train were edged with intricately patterned beading.

The corset-like back allowed the dress to be drawn in to emphasize one's figure beautifully.

Or it should have, anyway.

As soon as Penelope had pulled the laces tight, despite the women about me cooing their approval, I sensed something was wrong. Considering that all my clothing had fit perfectly thus far—though I had never been measured for so much as a nightgown—it was odd that the wedding dress and slippers fit like they had been commissioned for someone else, someone whose height and figure differed from mine.

"Not to worry, my lady," Penelope consoled, noting my consternation as I looked at the slippers, which were too small for my feet. "Suzy has a way with the needle, and she can put the dress to rights in no time. And I'm sure we can order another pair of slippers." Suzy, the plump maid with a penchant for humming, beamed at me as she prepared to make the necessary adjustments.

"The veil suits you," Penelope pronounced as she pinned the sheer fabric into place, allowing it to cascade down my back and puddle elegantly beyond the dress's train.

A slight uneasiness pulled at my stomach, incongruous with the nearly perfect picture of a bride in the mirror. Before I could ponder its meaning, the horde of women closed in, stripped me down, plopped me into a warm bath, and proceeded to scrub every inch of me until I glowed from head to toe, as pink and blemish-free as a newborn babe. My scalp was tender from the scouring, but that didn't stop the ladies from dragging combs through my hair to tame it into respectability as soon as they'd dried it. Wrapped in only my dressing gown, I bore the attentions with as little complaint as possible, but I began to lose patience as the process dragged on. It was all I could do to hold in the howls of abuse that were ringing through my mind. *And it's not even my wedding day!* I thought, shuddering as I imagined the fresh horrors awaiting me. As the maids continued to primp and prod, my mind conjured up images of battalions of determined young ladies, scouring brushes, greasy beauty creams, and enough ridiculous clothing to outfit a troupe of carnival folk. It would make any girl reconsider the merits of spinsterhood.

Hours later, I emerged from my room completely out of sorts with the world generally and the women of the household specifically, eager to put the whole experience behind me. But escaping notice seemed impossible. The staff buzzed with the news of my engagement, and everywhere I went I was warmly greeted and heartily congratulated. Even though they had only known me a short while, they were pleased that a serving maid could rise to such a level. Not wishing to spoil their romantic notions, I didn't mention that I was born to a respectable working-class gentleman rather than a life of servitude.

As I made my way through the throngs of well-wishers, I noted that once again, Jack was absent. Given our recent conversation, I was apprehensive to hear his opinion about my upcoming marriage to his friend. The rift between Jack and I might be irreparable, but my conscience wouldn't rest until we had spoken. I passed through the entire house, but I was unable to locate him. Thoroughly disgruntled, I sought out Philip instead.

"You look lovely, my darling," he said, at leisure in his favorite armchair in the library. He set his book aside, stood, and kissed me on the cheek.

"Hmmph," I grumbled. "When I pictured being pampered by lady's maids, I didn't imagine the experience would be quite so traumatizing."

His brows tented in concern. "Was it really that bad?"

"Yes," I said without hesitating. "They practically attacked me with pitchforks and axes."

A look of skepticism crossed his face.

"Fine, it wasn't exactly like that, but it was horrifying." I folded my arms over my chest.

He wrapped his arms around me, a tricky endeavor since I stubbornly kept my arms crossed. "Too much too soon?"

I held my tongue, not wishing him to interpret my frustration as a desire to be free from our engagement. "It seems . . . somewhat premature," I said, easing my rigid posture slightly. "We only became engaged last night."

"I'm sorry, my sweet," he said as he raised a hand to caress my cheek. "I can't seem to contain my excitement. Will you forgive my impatience?"

Those repentant gray eyes melted my resolve to remain irritated. I was far too susceptible to his charms. I felt my lips curve into a smile. "You make it difficult to stay upset, Philip," I murmured, slipping my hands around his waist to pull him closer.

"That's fortunate," he said, his lips a breath away from mine, "for marrying a fiery woman is a dangerous undertaking."

"Better a fiery wench than an ill-tempered bear in

trousers," I whispered wickedly, brushing my lips over his tauntingly.

"Be still, woman," he growled, silencing me with a kiss.

After a few minutes, I asked tentatively from my own armchair, "What other wedding plans have you made already?" Philip was seated at his desk, where he couldn't meddle with my emotions, distract me with caresses, or whisper sweet nothings that made my toes tingle.

He grinned rakishly before answering, and butterflies erupted in my stomach. Apparently, he could meddle with my emotions just as effectively from across the room. How annoying.

"Other than cleaning the house from top to bottom, I've charged the kitchen staff with preparing a wedding cake and a formal dinner, and I've directed the gardeners to give special attention to the grounds, especially the roses," he answered.

I kept myself from flinching at the mention of roses— the flowers always brought his childhood sweetheart to mind. Instead, I inquired, "And how long did you tell them they have to complete these tasks?"

"One week."

My breath caught in my throat. "One week?" I repeated with a squeak.

He couldn't keep the amusement off his face. "Too soon?"

"I . . . uh . . . ," I faltered, hunting for a valid reason, other than my fluttering nerves, to postpone the wedding.

"I've engaged the local priest for the day and sent word to your family. They should have plenty of time to arrive."

My chest constricted at the thought of seeing my family again, not to mention my imminent wedding. "It seems you've thought of everything," I managed in a semi-normal tone.

He left his chair to kneel beside me, taking my hand in his. "I know that tone, Bella. If it's not to your liking, you have only to name the date." He was offering to put my wishes before his. But the look of eagerness in his eyes, like a child itching to open his birthday presents but dutifully waiting for permission, was absolutely undeniable.

I held back the sigh I knew was about to pass my lips. "If it's what you really want . . ."

"It's everything I've ever wanted," he replied, leaning to kiss my hand and settling his head in my lap afterward.

"Then a week it is," I said, stroking his dark hair absently. The reality of my impending nuptials settled over me, and a strange uneasiness nestled in my stomach.

If I thought searching out Jack before had been a challenge, trying to do so between outings with Philip, dress fittings, going over wedding details with the staff, and opening box after box of items Philip had ordered from town was almost impossible. With only five days until the wedding and my family set to arrive at any time, I was determined to have every room in the house properly cleaned and aired out and the beds made up with fresh linens. Overseeing these tasks made me feel more useful, even if my involvement only irritated the housekeeper.

The only place that escaped severe cleaning was Rose's room. Secreted behind the tapestry, it remained untouched. I didn't wish to encroach on the home of Philip's former fiancée, even though it contained little more than dust and the belongings she'd left behind. It stood as a tribute to her memory, and though it nagged at me that it should stand empty, unwanted, and uncared-for, a certain sense of nostalgia kept me from sending the servants to tidy it up.

My room, however, was overrun with new dresses, riding gear, fine footwear, and more jewelry than I'd ever seen. It was all Penelope could do to keep everything in some semblance of order. I tried to convince Philip that it was too much, but the protests coming out of my mouth felt foreign. Hadn't I always wanted to be showered in beautiful things? Now it struck my newfound practicality as superfluous. My opinions, past or present, didn't seem to matter anyway; Philip refused to slow the constant flow of gifts.

I did enjoy orchestrating the comings and goings of the busy household. Sending servants on errands and collaborating with the head cook and housekeeper on menus and wedding plans was entirely to my liking. The role of mistress of the household fell easily on my shoulders, and I tackled every assignment energetically. Only thoughts of Jack kept me from fully appreciating the experience. The comfort of securing a man like Philip—the incarnation of everything I'd ever dreamed of—couldn't recompense the loss of my friend. After trying to corner Jack unsuccessfully several times, I approached Philip.

"Is Jack avoiding me?"

His gaze skittered away. "Nothing's wrong, if that's what you mean."

Thinking of stern schoolmistresses, I perched my hands on my hips and treated him to the steeliest of looks. "That's not precisely what I asked." When he didn't respond, I relaxed my stance and tried another tact. "Please, Philip. I haven't spoken to him in days. He's my friend. I just want to know what he makes of all this."

"'All this,' meaning . . . ?"

"The wedding, the changes to the household, everything. I want to speak to him, and he seems determined to keep me at a distance."

He sighed. "I know," he relented, running a hand through his hair. "I wish he would tell you himself."

"Tell me what?" I asked, sensing that something grave was coming.

His brow furrowed, but he finally met my eyes. "He's leaving."

"What?" A note of sharpness rang in my voice.

"He feels that with us starting a new life together, he would only be in the way. So he's heading out on his own."

The thought of the house forever devoid of Jack's company left me cold. There was no way I could admit this to my fiancé, so I said, "After all he's done for you, you're just going to let him go?"

He treated me to a pitying look. "I know, Bella. He's been a part of my life for as long as I can remember, but I can't make him stay. He put his life on hold for me when Rose left. I can't ask him to abandon his hopes for the future just for the comfort of having a friend nearby."

"Hopes for the future?" I repeated hollowly.

"Yes. He wants a wife, a home, and a family—just like everyone else. Just like I do." His voice was soft and entreating, his eyes full of tenderness as he gathered my hands in his.

Gently pulling my hands away, I folded them determinedly across my chest. I could see the logic of his words, though Jack's departure didn't sit well with me. "I suppose I'm not fond of losing those I care about." I didn't dare admit to myself—much less to Philip—how much I cared for Jack. "I just wish he could find his way here."

He took my face in his hands and gazed into my eyes. "I do too, my dear, but a man must find his own path in life. Jack has delayed long enough."

Allowing myself to get lost in his pale eyes, a portion of the sorrow I felt lessened at knowing Philip shared it. I slipped into his embrace and laid my head against his chest, needing its protection and safety. After a moment, I gathered the strength to ask the question I'd been avoiding. "When will he leave?"

"As soon as the wedding is over," he replied, stroking my hair soothingly.

My fingertips skimmed over the petals of a deep red rose, satiny smooth under my touch. The scent of the flowers, heady and fragrant, hung about the small rose garden. From bud to full bloom they tipped their faces upward like beautiful girls lifting their chins and awaiting admiration.

"How are they coming along?"

I tossed a glance at Philip. "You certainly seem to have a way with roses."

A grin spread across his face. "I do, don't I." Stepping up to me, his arms encircled my waist from behind. In silence, we watched the last of the day's sunrays, the clouds flushed orange-pink as they faded from the sky.

"Doesn't this feel like paradise?" I asked, basking in the beauty about me and breathing in the roses' perfume.

"Perfection," Philip murmured in my ear before placing a long kiss on my neck.

Even in the fading light, the jewel at my breast sparkled. I was to the point of adding that the only thing that made the moment more perfect was the fact that as man and wife we would always be together, when a movement out of the corner of my eye caught my attention. I flicked my eyes to the place and found Jack with a saddle cradled in his arms. Frozen in place, he watched us with his eyes full of sadness and the corners of his mouth pulled down. Jack and I stared at one another for a moment before he looked away, lifted his chin, hefted the saddle onto his shoulder, and strode toward the stable.

"Something wrong, Rose?" Philip's breath was warm on my neck when he spoke.

"No," I said quietly, my emotions tumbling about within me. "Everything is perfect."

The news of Jack's plans shook me more than I cared to admit; not only had it invaded my dreams, but it also spoiled my enjoyment of running the household. I busied myself with meaningless tasks, refusing to consider how his departure might affect me, though thoughts of him interrupted anything I tried to do. With less than three days before the wedding, I resolved to set the matter at rest by doing whatever was necessary to speak with him.

That was when I discovered the reason our paths hadn't crossed: he was keeping very strange hours, rising much earlier than everyone else and heading to bed hours after the entire household had retired. Watching out my window early in the morning, I found he was setting off on long rides before the sun rose and returning after breakfast to see to his duties when the household was busiest. With only two days until the wedding, I refused to let his stubbornness—or whatever was motivating his actions—keep me from speaking to him any longer, and I formulated a plan. Recalling with embarrassment how I'd barged into his room in little more than my dressing gown, I donned my most sensible dress, cloak, and shoes, and checked that my hair was neatly braided before heading outdoors before dawn. Waiting in the darkened stable, my ears strained for his footfalls as I rehearsed what I would say. At last, muted footsteps approached, and the stable door swung soundlessly open. All rational thought flew from my mind as it did so. He was little more than a broad-shouldered form against the predawn black, but there was no mistaking who it was.

"Good morning, Jack," I said.

Starting visibly, he took an involuntary step back, his hand flying to his chest.

A corner of my mouth curled up at his surprise. "Lovely day, isn't it?"

His hand dropped from his chest, and he released a long breath. "If one can indeed call this day."

I snickered, not realizing how I'd missed his dry humor. "I'm not the one who chose this time to be out and about. Generally, I prefer the comfort of my pillow at this hour."

He fumbled in the dark for a moment before a lantern hanging from a peg on the wall burst into life. In its low glow, Jack's face was a study in contrasts—his cheeks and brow burnished with light, while his eyes smoldered in the darkness, shadowed by thick rings. The reprimands I had rehearsed died on my lips. How many sleepless nights had he spent for it to be so plainly etched across his face? My heart softened, and without meaning to, I stepped forward.

He halted me with one upraised hand. "What is it, Bella?" he inquired warily, his eyes filled with unfathomable sadness.

I wanted to make a million confessions, a thousand clever observations, and a hundred scathing comments. All that came out was, "You're leaving."

He nodded slowly, his eyes on the ground. "I've been thinking about it for some time, and I believe it's for the best."

I wanted to wrap my arms around him, banish the sorrow from his face, and assure him that his place was with us. But the rigidity of his stance held me in place. Resigned, I settled onto a nearby barrel. "How is it best that you desert everyone you love? That was my plan too, remember? And it only resulted in heartache—until you and Philip stepped in."

He ran a hand through his hair agitatedly. "I can't stay here any longer."

"Why not?"

He let out a sigh and leaned on the stable wall, his shoulders stooped and his hands shoved into his pockets. "A couple starting out in life needs a chance to grow together. I don't want to stand in the way of that."

"But your place is here with us," I insisted. "Aren't you happy?"

The heavy circles under his eyes were proof that he was not. "It's not enough anymore. And now that Philip is finally settling down, it's my opportunity to see the world . . ." If his voice hadn't echoed so hollowly on the last phrase, and if I hadn't known how much he loved his home and his friend, and how much pride he took in his work here, I might have believed him.

"Since when has that been your goal?" I challenged, raising my eyebrows.

"What do you know of my ambitions, Bella?" There was no bitterness in his tone, and when his eyes met mine, I could sense no malice in them, only weariness.

"I know that you love this place and Philip more than you can express," I replied.

He nodded. "It's the only home I've ever known, and leaving will be the hardest thing I'll ever do. But I can't stay any longer."

"Then let me go with you." The plea slipped out before I could stop it. How could I say such a thing? I had a devoted fiancé ready to give me the world! How could I throw myself at this man's feet time and time again when all I'd ever met was rejection? Was I really that desperate?

Jack shook his head slowly. "No, Bella. Your place is at his side."

At this, the reservoir of fears inside me burst, spilling all the worries and frustrations I'd concealed so carefully—even from myself. Before I could stopper them up again, the worst of the fears gushed out. "What if it's all a mistake? What if I'm not meant to be with Philip?" Hot tears coursed down my cheeks as the words rattled out. "What if I don't love him enough?"

"You do," he assured me quietly, his gaze shifting up to meet mine. "And he loves you more each day."

"I've done nothing to merit his love. I'm just a petty child obsessed with *things*," I murmured through my tears. No matter how I had changed since I had left my family, I still felt like that child inside.

He shifted his weight, his hands twitching at his sides as though he were struggling against shackles and chains. With a look of determination, he pressed his back against the wall again, tucking his hands more firmly into his pockets. His voice, gentle as a caress, held all the reassurance I needed. "That may have been true once, Bella, but not anymore. You have become who you were meant to be." The words washed over me, warming me with their sincerity and stopping my tears. "Perhaps it's Philip who doesn't deserve you," he added softly.

Searching his face, I tried to grasp the meaning of his words. "Then who does deserve me?" I asked, watching him carefully.

One side of his mouth twitched, the first sign of good

humor I'd seen in him in a while. He shrugged. "Is anyone worthy of our Bella?"

Wiping tears away with a corner of my cloak, I said, "Now you sound like the overprotective father I never had."

"Then he didn't deserve you either," he said softly.

"You may tell him that yourself when you meet him." The full gravity of the situation fell upon me, and for the first time I imagined what the wedding would be like. My family would be at my side, and Philip—his eyes glowing with adoration—would stand across from me, my hands clasped in his. And Jack—where would he be? What expression would be painted across his face when I vowed to love and honor his best friend?

"Maybe I will."

My fanciful imaginings faded at Jack's serious tone, and silence crowded the space between us. Jack was the only one I could trust with my innermost fears; voicing my concerns to Philip would only crush him. "Do you really think I should marry him?" I asked at last.

He smiled sadly. "You are entitled to all of life's happiness, Bella. Who better to offer it to you than Philip?"

I held the words in for a heartbeat, rolling them over my tongue to fully taste them before releasing them. "Can you think of no one else?"

He held completely still, a statue half-dipped in light and shaded by darkness. His eyes flicked up to meet mine at last. "No," he said softly.

The part inside me that had been ruptured before was rent anew. I swallowed back the pain, blinking to keep the tears at bay and biting my lip to still its quivering. After a moment, I arose, summoning strength as I brushed off my skirts. Trying to keep the quaver from my voice, I said, "Then there's nothing more to say."

With an effort, I lifted my chin and made my way to the door, careful not to brush against him as I passed. But as I reached the threshold, his hand encircled my wrist, gently holding me back. I turned to him, fighting to keep my composure.

"I just want you to be happy, Bella," he said, his dark eyes reflecting the longing and misery I felt. Unable to stop myself, I grasped his shirtfront in both hands, dragging him closer and pressing my lips to his. For a second his mouth was hard as stone, and then his lips moved against mine, answering a need deep within me. His arms wrapped around me, crushing me to him. All the tension, frustration, and concern vanished with that kiss, and everything outside the two of us faded into unimportance for one perfect moment. When he finally pulled away to look into my face, I could feel his heart beating under my hands. My lips buzzed from the pressure of his mouth on mine.

My breath caught in my throat at the emotions written so plainly across his face: passion, devotion, love. How could I have ever doubted his feelings for me? The truth was penned in every look, every word, and every kindness he had rendered. My heart soared at the revelation.

"I want you to be happy, Bella," he reiterated slowly, shattering the silence and bringing me back to reality with a mental thump. "And your best chance is with Philip. He needs you." His words were soft and imploring, as warm as his arms around me. "He can give you everything you ever wanted. Don't you understand? I could never do that." One hand moved up to my cheek, cupping it gently. He gazed into my eyes for a moment, his face a study in torment from the downturned mouth to the eyes full of untold hopelessness, before placing a lingering kiss on my forehead. "Good-bye, Bella." He released me from his embrace and walked past me and out the half-opened door.

Alone in the dim stable, I stared out into the darkness where Jack had disappeared. A shiver washed over me as a breeze snuffed out the lamp. Goose bumps erupted all over my arms, and I rubbed at them futilely. Their presence had nothing to do with the temperature and everything to do with the shard of ice that had taken up residence where my heart should have been.

The day dawned clear and bright, and the household exuded more cheerfulness than ever. The wedding was two days away, and my family would arrive before nightfall, allowing me only a few hours to grieve for Jack. I sent Penelope away, claiming to have a throbbing headache. It was true enough, given the early morning I had spent in wakeful misery.

The real ailment, I knew, was less physical. My mind kept conjuring up memories of Jack—the mingled adoration and sorrow in his eyes, the passion of his embrace, and the frenzy of his kiss. That kiss had touched a place in me Philip had never been able to reach. It had shaken me to my very core, bringing clarity and understanding; it had been tantamount to a declaration of love.

He's leaving, I reminded myself. Whether he

reciprocated my feelings or not, he had made it clear that he had no intention of acting upon them. Tears of frustration and misery burned down my cheeks, leaving my throat thick, my eyes raw, and my insides feeling as if they'd been scooped out. Reliving the scene over and over caused the ice in my heart to spread until I wondered if I would ever be warm again.

"Bella?" A strong palm rested on my brow, testing for fever before brushing the hair from my forehead. In my sleep-deprived state, I wondered if it was Father, soothing me as he had when I suffered from childhood illnesses. Cracking open an eye, I found Philip perched on the edge of my bed, concern furrowing his brow.

I wanted to assure him that I was fine, that everything was wonderful. I longed to promise him that the wedding would be perfect and that we would live happily ever after. But the words didn't make it past the lump in my throat, and the flow of tears I thought I had exhausted in the night coursed down my cheeks again.

Without a word, Philip scooped me up in his arms, blankets and all, and held me against his chest while he rocked me back and forth. Gradually, the tightness in my chest began to ease, his tenderness stilling the ache inside. I freed a hand from the tangle of blankets to stroke his cheek, smooth from this morning's shave. His eyes, alight with love, met mine.

"I'm sorry," I whispered softly, tracing the line of his jaw with a fingertip. I wanted to explain why I was sorry—for my feelings for Jack, for betraying Philip's love, and for this horrible display days before our wedding. The words wouldn't come.

He pulled me closer, placing a kiss on my brow. "Cold feet, my love?" His lips curved into a slight grin. "As I understand, they're fairly common."

My mood lightened, the frozen lump inside me momentarily forgotten. I followed his lead. "So you're having cold feet?" More than anything, I wanted him to say yes, that he, too, had reservations and was nervous about what was coming.

"Not in the least."

My disappointment in his response was short-lived; Philip's lips found mine, distracting me with a series of gentle kisses. I struggled not to remember Jack's kiss, wild and passionate, the emotions inside me roiling with his. Philip's kisses didn't shake me the way Jack's had, but they calmed me just the same.

"After all," Philip added, "I'm getting everything I want." That was Jack's wish—that Philip and I both have everything we wanted. The expression on Jack's face as he abandoned me in the stable rushed back to me. His face was caught in the lamplight, and the hopelessness he'd tried to hide was revealed before he retreated into the darkness. Jack was sacrificing everything for his friends. The tears—*would they never end?*—pricked at my eyes. I swallowed them back and focused on Philip— kind, sweet, loving Philip, who was ready to carry me off and make all my dreams come true.

"You're too good for me," I choked out, fresh tears blurring my vision.

"Impossible. Nothing's too good for you. I only hope to one day be worthy of you, Bella." That declaration only further reminded me of Jack, and I struggled to swallow back more sobs. Philip kissed the tears away, then covered my mouth with his, the tang of salt sharp on our lips. He released me at last, but I clung to him, feeling tossed on a turbulent sea of emotion, craving his strength to keep me from going under.

"Is there anything else troubling you?" A deeper fear flickered in his eyes.

I hurried to reassure him. "Like you said, nothing but cold feet," I sniffled, unable to bear it if he knew the truth. Someday I might tell him—reveal the folly of my misplaced affections—but for now, I could only suppress them and do my best to move forward.

The black carriage rolled slowly up the drive, trailing an ominous gray cloud. The angle made it hard to see inside, but my stomach twisted with apprehension just the same. Philip's fingers found mine, warming and squeezing them. He gave no sign of the nerves that held me captive. Head erect and shoulders thrown back, he stood beside me on the front steps, garbed in his second-best suit—a nearly black gray that made his eyes pop, a white shirt and cravat, and his shiny coal-black boots. If I hadn't been so intent on the carriage creeping closer, I might have taken more time to appreciate just how attractive he looked.

On top of everything, the individual poised stiffly on the other side of Philip kept catching my attention as well. I refused to look at Jack, who seemed to be just as studiously avoiding looking at me. Philip, on the other hand, was not only confident but perfectly obliging, well-mannered, and hospitable. There was certainly nothing of the Beast in him today. He had completely transformed from the first time I had met him. The creature that had skulked and brooded was nowhere to be found.

When the wheels creaked to a halt, Philip was at the carriage door before the footman could jump into action. Jack and I hung back and watched the door swing open. My father was the first to emerge, his brow knit into a tight line. A dam burst within me and I threw myself into his arms almost before his feet touched the ground. Tears flowed down my cheeks as I clung to him, safe in his embrace. The smell of wood that always hung about him enveloped me. He held me tightly and stroked my hair. "I'm so sorry, my dear," he murmured.

I pulled away to look him in the face, my arms still around him. "I'm the one who's truly sorry, Father . . ." Now that it came to the point, I couldn't find the words to explain my remorse any better than that, but he seemed to require no further confession. "I've missed you all so much," I said after a moment, burying my face in his chest again.

By this time, Cassie and Aaron had descended from the carriage and were standing politely to one side. One glance at Cassie's expression of discomfort was enough to convince me that she was the same kind sister as always, and without thinking, I pulled her into an embrace. Her tears wet my cheeks as she apologized over and over until I hushed her.

"I'm just happy to see you again," I said sincerely. "I didn't appreciate everything you did until I had to do it myself. How did you stay calm in the face of endless days of cooking and cleaning?"

She let out a snuffly, tearful laugh. "I have no doubt you did admirably. You always excelled at anything you put your mind to."

It was my turn to laugh, remembering my consternation at doing the men's laundry and the argument over Philip's haircut. "Undoubtedly you would have handled things better."

"Impossible," she beamed at me, giving me a sisterly squeeze. "No one is as bright and resourceful as my sister."

I smiled. "If that is true, I know where I learned it. Your good sense, resourcefulness, and patience have been my guide in this new life."

Swiping tears from her eyes with the back her hand, she said, "We should never have sent you away."

"Everything worked out," I assured her. "And now we are here together. All is forgiven." I hugged her again, attempting to inject all the love and regret I felt into the embrace.

We broke apart at last. I cast my gaze on Aaron, who was still standing apart with his eyes downcast, nervously gouging a hole in the earth with one boot. "Little brother," I said, stepping up to him to throw my arms about him. He was my same tall, skinny, younger brother—all sharp angles and height. He surprised me by returning my hug with gusto, nearly crushing me in the process.

He whispered a husky apology against my ear, but swallowed up in my family's love as I was, I just shook my head and smiled up at him to assure him that all was forgiven. Breaking away from Aaron, but keeping his hand in mine and capturing Cassie's with the other, I turned to face Philip and Jack. Philip was sporting a wide grin, and even Jack's uneasy expression had lightened.

I stepped forward, remembering my place as soon-to-be mistress of the house. "Father," I said politely, "This is Philip."

I had discovered that not only had Philip sent word to my family of the upcoming wedding, he also had included a lengthy description of what had occurred since my arrival and had begged both for my father's forgiveness as well as permission to wed his daughter. What I didn't know was how this letter had been received.

My father squinted at his host for a moment, probably trying to catch a glimpse of the Beast he had met in the man before him. Finally, he reached forward and gripped Philip's outstretched hand in a hearty handshake. "Thank you for taking care of my little girl," he said, the pride in his tone warming my heart and settling my nerves.

"My honor, sir," Philip replied with a slight bow of his head. "May I present my steward, Jack?" he added, waving Jack forward. The two shook hands warmly.

"Philip, this is my elder sister, Cassandra." Philip bowed over her hand prettily, and her cheeks flushed. Lovely as she was, Cassie had never grown accustomed to the attentions of handsome men.

"It's a pleasure to meet you," she managed. Somehow, this interchange bothered me less than when, a moment later, Jack was introduced to her and kissed her hand in greeting, causing her blush to deepen. Some foul beastie within me demanded I throw her across the yard and well out of his sight, but I took a steadying breath and introduced Philip to Aaron instead.

One eyebrow raised, Philip looked Aaron over for an extra second, undoubtedly remembering that this was the individual who had taken the lead in throwing me out of my home. Aaron, bearing the scrutiny as bravely as possible, swallowed nervously. Then Philip grabbed him by the hand and pulled him into a tight hug, patting him vigorously on the back. "Thank you, Aaron," he said. "Without your actions, Bella never would have left the house." Surprised by the interchange, I laughed aloud, and my father's deep chuckle echoed mine.

The reunion and introductions completed, Philip took me by the hand. Facing my family, he announced, "You are all most welcome to our home. As you are all likely famished, lunch is ready. Jack, would you lead us in?"

Jack offered his elbow to Cassie, who, having recovered her composure, slid her arm through his, smiled shyly, and gazed up at him through golden lashes. My heart plummeted. That was the same smile that had captured hearts for miles around Stohl and Stanton. It was just as well Jack was leaving. I couldn't bear to have him court my sister.

Philip squeezed my hand, drawing my attention as the pair led the way into the house, followed by Aaron and my father. Philip held me back a moment longer so that our voices wouldn't be overheard. "That went well, don't you think?" he asked, his eyes alight with optimism.

"Yes," I admitted. "Much better than I imagined, in fact."

"And Jack and Cassandra? What do you make of that?"

he commented, his eyes trailing after her lithe form. "She's certainly as beautiful as you claimed."

Reaching up, I twisted his chin until our eyes met. My lips pulled into a tight line, and I shook my head slowly from side to side.

"Right. Sorry, my love," he said quickly, planting a brief kiss on my cheek. "Shall we go in?"

The meal was a relatively simple affair—certainly less grand than our dinners were—but the food was filling, the conversation entertaining, and the company the best. The occasion was marred only by Jack's pointed attentions to Cassie and Cassie's alluringly sweet smiles in response. Their flirtatious behavior got under my skin, and I prayed that Jack's resolve to leave would hold out in light of this new development. It took all of Philip's solicitousness, my father's kindly observations, and Aaron's jibes to keep me from flinging the tray of sandwiches at my sister's head.

When the ordeal finally ended, I found myself whisked upstairs, arm-in-arm with none other than Cassie. "You must show me all your things!" she said in an uncharacteristic display of excitement. Cassie, ever occupied with the care of the household—weaving cloth to sell at market, planning and preparing the family's meals—spared little time for admiring pretty things. She made up for this in full as she rifled through the expensive gowns, shoes, and jewelry that Philip had gifted me. Taking advantage of her momentary distraction, I broached the subject that was bothering me.

"Jack seems quite taken with you," I commented nonchalantly as she tried on some of my jewelry at the mirror.

"He's just being polite," she replied, trying the effect of sapphire earrings with the pendant she had clasped around her throat. "I'm sure he means nothing by it."

Her response allayed my concerns only slightly. I pushed the issue further, just to be sure. "All the same, it's clear he admires you greatly."

"No," she clipped the earrings on. "He's like all the others." She waved a hand, as if the adoring men who had come to call over the years were arranged before her and she was dismissing them one and all. "Philip, on the other hand," she added with a mischievous tilt to her lips, "I'd steal him from you in a minute, Bella. He's much more attractive."

Comparing Philip's towering height and classic good looks with Jack, I had to admit that Cassie was right. But there was something I didn't like about the comment just the same. Perhaps it was how readily she had admitted that, given the chance, she would steal my fiancé. However, I begrudgingly admitted to myself, it might also have been the way she discounted Jack without another thought. *There is so much* more *to him!* I wanted to argue. Philip was tall, handsome, charming, and well-mannered, but Jack possessed a kindness and humor that reached my very soul. I shook my head, attempting to dispel the thoughts of Jack that kept settling there.

An unhappy look crossed Cassie's face as she replaced the earrings and necklace in the jewelry box. She had always been quick to perceive others' feelings. "I'm sorry, Bella. I don't know why I said that." She squeezed both my hands and looked into my eyes. "You are happy, aren't you?"

The question took me aback. "Of course," I replied automatically. "Philip is everything I ever wanted. He's handsome, distinguished, and wealthy, and he adores me. What more could I ask for?" It was exactly what I had been telling myself all along, but nevertheless my heart continued to ache.

"Philip is perfect," she said. "I'm sure you'll have a wonderful life together." I could see something else lingering in her eyes before she put it into words. "I can't believe he was ever any different."

This was a subject I could address without any pangs to my conscience. "You would have believed it if you'd seen it firsthand. Though he has changed for good, I think." I added, "There are times when I miss the person I could so easily boss around and rail at. I can't find it in me to treat Philip like that anymore." This last sentiment was something I had been struggling with for a while. There were moments when I missed the Beast's stubborn grumpiness, even in the face of Philip's generous, loving attitude. It was a stone on which I could sharpen my wit. *Does nothing of the Beast remain?* I wondered for the millionth time.

Cassie laughed softly. "I imagine you do. I'm sure you enjoyed bossing him around." I laughed in chorus with her. She knew me too well.

At this very moment, she spied my wedding dress, hung carefully at the back of the closet. Pulling it forward, she said, "Its perfect, Bella—so elegant and stately. Won't you try it on for me?" She held it out, and the hope gleaming in her eyes left me no choice. I hadn't tried on the gown since Suzy had completed the alterations, and I had only put on the slippers and veil once. To see the effect of all three took my breath away.

"You're stunning," Cassie said softly. Standing behind me, she gazed into the mirror, her eyes shining with approbation. Careful not to dislodge the veil, she wrapped her arms around my shoulders in a sisterly embrace. "I'm so proud of you, little sister," she whispered, resting her warm cheek against mine.

The moment was everything I'd hoped for when I'd imagined our reunion—full of love and mutual appreciation. I wanted to confide everything in her, and suddenly the effort of holding back the barrage of words, doubts, and fears was too much.

What would she think of me, in love with Jack but marrying Philip instead? Tears rolling down my face, I pulled away, sat down on the bed, and buried my face in my hands. Without missing a beat, Cassie retrieved a handkerchief and passed it to me.

"What is it, Bella?" she asked, always ready to comfort a wounded soul.

I blew my nose before offering up the same excuse I'd given Philip. "Just wedding nerves. Do you think I could have a moment to pull myself together?"

"Of course. Take all the time you need," she responded. "I'll be close by if you want me," she said before slipping quietly out the door.

Mopping my cheeks with the handkerchief, I looked down at my lap, swathed in the expensive satin of my wedding gown, with the tips of my elegant slippers peeping out below the beaded hem. I stared at the intricate pattern of the beading, trying to regain my composure. As happens when one stares absentmindedly at a picture, something suddenly shifted, and everything came into focus. I gasped as I realized what the trailing lines of beads and embroidery represented, and at the same moment, a vision burst upon me.

Fifteen

A room littered with boxes of all sizes spread before me, gorgeous gowns, jewelry, and fine slippers pouring out of them. Philip, sitting beside me on the bed, held a box far larger than all the rest. His eyes were alight with boyish excitement as he thrust it into my hands.

"Is this . . . ?" I began.

"Open it and see," he replied, struggling to suppress his exuberance.

Savoring the look on his face, I took my time sliding off the lid. Yards of white fabric met my eye. My wedding gown, I thought, a delicious thrill running up my spine. I pulled forth the dress, my fingertips rubbing against the smooth material. Small sleeves, fully beaded with tiny pearls, accented the plain bodice. The full skirt was edged with more beading in a repeating pattern. I felt my lips curve into a grin as I recognized the design.

"Are those . . . ?"

"Roses," he assented, beaming proudly. With one long finger, he traced the petals of one bloom, its leaves and stem intertwining with the next.

"It's beautiful," I replied, a knot forming in my throat. Unshed tears stung my eyes as I looked at the exquisite gown in my lap. A multitude of lovely things surrounded me, and now this, the loveliest of all. The conversation with Jack came back to me, and tears slipped down my cheeks. I questioned for the first time if it was enough to justify the sacrifice I was making.

"What is it, Rose?" Philip asked plaintively. Placing his palms on my cheeks, he lifted my face until our eyes met, wiping my tears with his thumbs.

I didn't want to say it. I didn't want to be the woman who threw away everything good in her life for a girlhood fancy, but abandoning my dreams was equally unbearable— it would leave me regretful for the rest of my life. Swallowing nervously, I said, "What if we were to postpone the wedding?"

"Postpone the . . . ," he began, obviously stunned. "I don't understand," he said slowly. "I thought this was what you wanted. What we both wanted."

"It is," I assured him, covering his hand with one of mine. "I love you, Philip, more than I can say. But what about my dreams?"

Confusion spread over his face. "Your dreams?" he repeated.

"Yes," I said, guilt filling me for springing this on him now of all times, less than a month before our wedding. "My music. I've been speaking with a music master in town, and he thinks that with the right training—"

"And you would postpone our wedding for this?" Disapproval gleamed in his eyes, and though he tried to hide it, a slight edge of scorn flavored his tone.

"Just for a few months—a year at most. Then I would know if there was any chance of success," I hastened to reply, "and we could start a family,"

He pulled his hands from mine, his eyes narrowing. "A year." Leaning away from me, he crossed his arms over his chest. The youthful exuberance of a moment before had disappeared from his face, the line of his jaw rigid. "And why is this the first time I've heard of this? Isn't all of this enough for you?" He waved to the room full of expensive things.

"It isn't that . . . ," I faltered.

"Then I'm not enough for you? Is that it?" The disdain in his voice lashed out at me like a physical blow. This was a side of Philip I had rarely seen. Even when his temper got the better of him, he would be meek as a lamb the next minute, begging forgiveness for his actions. A million childhood moments flashed though my mind in proof, but at the moment, everything in his stance indicated a barely controlled rage, the likes of which I had never witnessed before.

"No!" The word was louder than I would have liked, but the change in his demeanor had unsettled me. I lowered my voice carefully. "You don't understand—"

"Here is what I understand, Rosalind," he interrupted, his arms still crossed tightly over his chest and his expression thunderous. "Years of working and planning together, and you are prepared to throw it all away on a whim."

Now I was angry. To misunderstand was one thing, but to willfully twist my words and throw them back at me was another. My veins buzzed with righteous ire. I rose to my feet, not caring that the gown crumpled to the floor as I did so. "My dreams are not a whim!" I retorted. "If you can't comprehend that, perhaps we shouldn't be married after all!"

"Maybe we shouldn't!" he replied, rising to glower down at me before storming out the door. He paused on the threshold, one hand clutching the doorframe, and without looking back, he said, "You are not the woman I thought you were, Rose."

The world crashed down around my ears, my heart shattered into a million pieces, and tears of anger and sorrow burned down my cheeks. I stared mutely at the empty doorway and planned what I would do next.

Darkness fell. Shoving the most precious items into a large satchel and checking to be sure the jewel was in place at my throat, I slipped noiselessly out of the home I had known since my youth. As the tang of the forest trees met me, I remembered that in my haste I had left no note to explain why I had left or where I was headed. Night breezes whipped my dark curls into my face as I wondered if I would ever see Jack or Philip again.

My mind reeled with images of Rose ready to burst with anger, packing the few items she couldn't bear to part with and disappearing into the night, never to be seen again by her loved ones. Finally, I understood why Rose had left and never returned—partly to chase after her dreams, but mostly to escape Philip.

I looked down at the dress. The reality that it had been hers was difficult to accept. How dare he put me in her wedding gown? Was I nothing better than a shadow of his former love? Did he see me as nothing more than her replacement? A portion of the anger that had driven Rose away thrummed through my veins as I thought about the vision. Rose, regretful and scared, and Philip, angrier than either of us had seen him. *The Beast*, the voice at the back of my mind provided, *He became the Beast in that moment.* Ill treatment was to be expected from such a creature, but Philip's gentility made one believe in his show of goodness. With growing fury, I wondered if he had ever truly changed, or if kindness was a lie he plastered on his handsome face each day. Bitter disappointment weighed my heart down. Combined with mounting indignation, a truly frightening rage took hold of me. Without thinking, I stalked down to Philip's study, and flung the door open, not caring if it banged against the wall and informed the entire household of my foul mood.

"Bella?" Philip said, startled. His black brows flew up, then drew into a line of concern as he noted my tight-lipped expression. "What is it?"

"This, for one," I said, wrenching the veil from my head and hurling it in his direction. "And these!" Pulling the slippers from my feet, I launched them one at a time at his head. He ducked out the way easily, which only infuriated me further.

"What is this about?" he asked again, a fraction of the Beast's impatience creeping into his voice.

"Did they belong to her as well?" I demanded, glaring at him.

"Did they belong to whom?" he asked, irritation evident in his tone.

"This was her dress, wasn't it? Are you planning to tart me up in all your former fiancée's clothing to make believe she never left you?" I challenged.

He returned my glare with a measure of the Beast's

familiar anger as he growled, "You have no idea what you're talking about."

"As a matter of fact, I do," I replied coldly, crossing my arms over my chest and sticking out my chin.

Mirroring my attitude, he folded his arms over his chest and leaned back in his chair, regarding me coldly. "Is that so?" His voice was low, a tone I knew heralded danger.

"You drove that poor girl away! And now you've maneuvered me into her place!" My chest heaving, I took a stabilizing breath, reigned in my fury slightly, and lowered my voice like he had. "I have something to say to you, Philip: no amount of gifts or fancy clothing can bring Rose back or turn me into her. She's gone, and she'll never return. Understand that once and for all." I gave him my steeliest gaze yet, to ensure that he caught my next words. "And I, for one, don't blame her." With that I reached up and, with one deft twist, broke the chain encircling my throat and hurled the ruby pendant to the floor. "I have only one more thing to say: I have never loved you, and I will never marry you."

Tears of rage poured down my face, obstructing my vision as I shut the door behind me. How could anyone cry so much and still find tears to shed? A sense of triumph—tempered by the lead in my heart at the thought of what I had just done—propelled me down the hallway. Blindly, I stumbled on, my feet halting in front of a familiar tapestry. Of course. Something had always whispered to me that this is where I would end up someday. It was where I belonged.

Hands shaking, I thrust aside the tapestry and wrenched the doorknob behind it. Pressing my weight against the door, I heaved until it gave way. I tumbled into the room as I had done before, falling to my knees as a cloud of dust enveloped me. The door swung shut of its own accord, leaving me alone in the forgotten room.

I gave way to my emotions then. Rage, frustration, and disappointment shook my frame. The bodice of the wedding gown, smeared with grime where I'd fallen, was soon blotched with tears as well. Why should I care? It had never been mine. Like Philip, it had been meant for another—the woman he'd never stopped loving, regardless of his amorous declarations to me. Everything I fooled myself into believing lay shattered at my feet. My love for Philip had been a farce—mere infatuation blended with a vestige of Rose's feelings. Likewise, his love for me had been no more than a pale reflection of his devotion to his childhood sweetheart.

And Jack? Why hadn't I fought against his resolve to abandon me to Philip? I had seen the love so plainly in his eyes, as fierce and strong as mine for him. But what right had I to his love? In my ignorance, I had thrown away the affections of a kind family, the care of a real friend, the adoration of a fiancé, and the chance to have the life I had always imagined.

Love had been meaningless to me once. Like the cheapest of currencies, I had liberally bartered and traded it for goods and services. Now, with nothing but disappointed hopes and a future devoid of even the barest glimmer of affection, all I could think about was how much love I had frittered away.

I had come full circle, landing in the same predicament as Rose. Looking around me at the room she had known as a girl, I saw her neatly made bed, her dresses meticulously arranged in the closet, and her tarnished hair clips littering the vanity. Other than the thick film of dust blanketing everything, it was exactly as she had left it. It was as if the room itself awaited her return with an air of watchful anticipation. I wanted to shout—like I had at Philip—that she was never coming back, but the gray walls would only stare accusingly back at me, exactly as Philip had done. This room, disused and neglected, served only as a dreary reminder of her unfulfilled ambitions, hopes, and loves.

I wanted to cast blame on Rose for setting the trap I had walked into, on my family for not curbing my behavior early on in life, on my mother for abandoning me to a cruel world when I was little more than a toddler, and on Jack for withholding his love.

But in the end, I knew I only had myself to blame.

The realization was too much to bear. Something inside me snapped. With one broad movement, I swept the contents of the vanity to the floor, enjoying the tinkling sounds as the combs and pins knocked against one another before coming to rest in the thick dust. Looking into the mirror, a mad woman—wild-eyed and garbed in Rose's soiled wedding dress—met my gaze. With a mighty shove, I dislodged the gilt-edged mirror from its place. The glass shattered with a satisfying crunch as it joined the debris on the floor. The bedding, already in a poor state, was next. Grabbing handfuls, I threw the coverlet and sheets on the floor and reached for the pillows.

Within moments, musty feathers drifted through the air. Fueled by rage and eager to wreak more havoc, I turned to the closet. Feeling a wicked sort of glee at seeing Rose's lovely things reduced to rubbish, I yanked dresses from their places and ripped them to shreds until they all covered the floor in a tangled heap.

I came to myself then, appalled at what I had done. The once lovely room, regal as an ancient queen, was ruined. Would this be my fate? Was I to be neglected and abandoned as well, waiting in hopeful silence for a future that would never arrive? Collapsing atop the remains of Rose's clothing, I buried my face in the torn material on the closet floor, grieving for all I had lost and for what I had become.

Sixteen

When the tears had finally abated and numbness replaced my turbulence, I raised my head to survey the wreckage. Ragged strips of fabric, a mangled mass of hairpins and brushes, and shattered glass glinting like diamonds covered the floor. The chamber that had once been so lovely was now little more than a cautionary tale to vain ambition, a sad memorial to unrealized hopes and joys.

Like me.

Grimly, I pondered my fate. My own ambitions, like Rose's, were dashed beyond repair. No matter what had occurred in the past, I had never abandoned my dreams— not when my family had deserted me, not on my worst days as a servant in the Beast's household with my hands cracked and aching, not when I had filled the kitchen with smoke from yet another bulbous loaf of burnt bread, and not even when Jack had made my heart soar before abandoning me. Not even then had I given up on the deepest wishes of my heart.

A good life, filled with love and prosperity, would one day be mine. *It must*, I assured myself, believing with stubborn tenacity that the universe could not be so cruel as to deny me everything I longed for. "The darkest hour comes just before the dawn"—the worn-out adage had always comforted me, even when disappointment upon disappointment had been heaped upon me. I had never stopped believing in its truth—until now.

The afternoon light fading, I let go of my fondest dreams, allowing the glimmer of hope that had always burned inside of me to sputter and wink out as Rose's room fell into shadow. How long I watched the dimness swallow up the rubble, covering its ugliness in softest gray, I couldn't say. I wished for a similar reprieve from my own misdeeds, but remaining here in the darkness only delayed the inevitable.

Philip would not take me back, and even if by some miracle he did, nothing would ever be the same. I couldn't allow myself to return to my old roles, either as his servant or his lover. Jack had rejected me twice already, and I refused to humiliate myself a third time by throwing myself on his mercy. My family, well-acquainted with my follies, would be too embarrassed by my recent behavior to intervene, and rightly so. Without a doubt, they would draw quietly away, leaving me to my own devices. Who could blame them? I had brought this upon myself, and now I had to swallow my pride and find the solution, whatever the cost. I racked my brain for a way to escape with a shred of dignity intact.

It came to me as I thought of my sister and all she had done for me. Hadn't Cassie been content to work along-side Father to create a home for us? Laboring with all her might, she'd served and protected those in her care without consideration for her own happiness. No better example of patient sacrifice existed in the whole world.

Could I do the same? I had found a sense of purpose in tending to my household duties as the Beast's servant, and I'd learned the value of being useful. Surely I could find a position in some far-off household and put my talents to use. Calmness settled over me as I contemplated a new life, filled with caring for others and bettering their lives. There was a certain nobility in serving kindly and well, no matter how it was accomplished.

Rose, whose plight so closely mirrored mine, flitted through my thoughts. I wondered if she had gone through the same process, ruling out her options until only one remained. Had she thought it would be best for everyone if she disappeared without a trace? She had been sorely mistaken, and I wondered if, wherever she had gone, she regretted that decision. Now that I had come to esteem them so highly, I could not bear to leave my friends and family without begging for their forgiveness and bidding them a proper farewell. Then, this part of my life could gently come to a close as another opened. In the fresh chapter about to unfold, I vowed to face reality head-on and not lose myself to daydreams or girlish fancies, but to go about my duties with my vision clear and my head held high. Sitting up, I wrapped my arms around my knees, accepting my fate. The last of the day's light faded from the sky, leaving the room wrapped in darkness.

The door creaked open, and light spilled through the entryway. A set of booted feet trod through the refuse, glass cracking under each footfall. Holding my breath, I watched the boots progress through the tattered clothing, torn bed coverings and other rubbish until they came to a halt in front of me. Lamp in hand, the visitor squatted down to peer at me. Light poured over his face.

Jack.

My heart leapt to my throat. The lamplight revealed an expression of pity, sorrow, and other emotions that made my mind balk. Drowning in a sea of humiliation, I ducked my head and threw an arm over my face to hide from his view. But my curiosity, as unquenchable as ever, made me peek out from the crook of my elbow.

After a moment, he fit his large frame into the unoccupied space beside me in the closet, setting the lamp carefully between us. "I haven't been in this room for years," he mused, looking around. "Charming, isn't it?"

How could he make jokes at a time like this? So typical.

"It appears that someone threw a perfect fit," he observed, lifting a scrap of ginger-hued fabric, the lamplight wavering over its glossy grain. "I don't blame you for destroying this dress, though. It looked perfectly hideous on her."

I snorted, clapping a hand over my mouth as soon as the sound rushed out.

"Ah, signs of life," he said, turning his attention back to me and dropping the piece of cloth. "After this afternoon's tirade, I thought you'd come in here to die quietly." One corner of his mouth tilted up. "Or," he amended, "perhaps not so quietly."

"It seems I was unsuccessful," I muttered.

A wry grin curved his mouth. "Are you sure you gave it your best effort? As much effort as you devoted to redecorating this space, for instance?"

I knew his ribbing would continue until I put an end to it, so I lifted my head to look at him fully. "That wasn't exactly my plan."

He gazed back at me, wordless.

"Though I considered it." His eyebrows rose. "Not dying," I clarified, "but going quietly out of your life."

His eyebrows lowered, rumpling into a furrow. He turned to the room around us. "That's what she did, you know—she passed quietly out of our lives. And look where that got us." The humor was gone from his voice.

Recalling the pain Rose's disappearance had caused him, I sat up straighter, placed my elbows on my knees and rested my chin on my palms. "I would never have left without saying good-bye," I said quietly. "But I can't stay here any longer. It's time for me to make my own way in the world, Jack." It was the same explanation he had used, and it felt just as paltry coming out of my own mouth.

He seemed to be pondering what I'd said, his face taking on a thoughtful quality. "What if there's another way?"

"Another way?"

"You told me my place was here, in this household, with those I love." Jack's eyes were on me, watching me anxiously as he spoke. "Now I'm here to tell you the same."

"It won't work," I replied, fatigue flavoring my words. "I don't love Philip enough to make a life with him."

The corner of his mouth twitched, creating a brief smile line that disappeared as quickly as it appeared. "The entire household is aware of that," he said. "You didn't exactly express yourself quietly."

At least someone found my disgrace amusing.

"But then, you wouldn't be Bella if you kept things to yourself," he added.

Mildly frustrated, I responded, "I was angry. It doesn't excuse my behavior, but it doesn't make what I said any less true. I can't live a lie."

He surprised me by responding, "I know."

I looked him over, noting the seriousness in his eyes and in the tight line of his mouth. "Then what do you propose?" I finally asked, lifting my chin to meet his eyes fully.

"If you could stay without marrying Philip—"

"And do what exactly, serve as his scullery maid?" Even though I had been considering a similar situation, the idea of returning to my old role in *this* household didn't appeal to me. Instead of embracing the future and striding into the great unknown, it would be a step backward.

"No," he said, choosing his words with great care. "In a much different capacity."

I was at a loss. "Such as . . . ?"

His hands fidgeted in his lap, an uncharacteristic manifestation of nervousness. After a long hesitation, he replied, "The steward's wife?"

I sat up straighter, unable to believe his words. "Are you proposing to me, Jack?"

A rueful grin appeared on his face.

My heart thumping wildly, I closed my eyes and leaned back against the closet wall, breathing slowly and trying to gather my wits. "You want to marry me?" I asked again, opening my eyes to read the expression on his face. Another thought occurred to me, putting a damper on my newfound hope. "What about Cassie?"

"Your sister?" he asked. "What does she have to do with—"

"You seemed . . ." I pushed the words out, hating them even as I did so. ". . . quite taken with her."

He shook his head dismissively, then tipped it to the side, as if contemplating another aspect of the situation. "Strange you should bring her up, though . . ." The silence lengthened as he gathered his thoughts, my inquisitiveness kept in check only with great effort. "It seems Cassie might be the key to solving our little dilemma," he said at last.

"Dilemma?" I parroted, digesting his words. Cassie would make a much better wife for Jack. She was kind and hardworking, willing to labor beside him without complaint. Undoubtedly, she would volunteer to muck out the stables. In a tiny voice, I asked, "So you do fancy her?"

He cast me an assessing glance, his eyes flitting over my face before flicking away. "Not in the way you're suggesting. My heart was already spoken for when she arrived." He fixed his dark eyes on me. They were buttery warm in the low light.

I wanted more than anything to bask in their warmth, but I had to make sure the affection I saw there was mine alone. "Rose?" I asked timidly.

He shook his head, keeping his eyes trained on me the whole time so I couldn't miss his meaning. Relief washed over me, but his comment nagged at me, piquing my curiosity. "Exactly what dilemma are you referring to?"

He slung an arm around my shoulders, pulling me against him in a comradely fashion. "Everyone's mixed-up affections, Bella. You thought you loved Philip and he thought he loved you, when in actuality he had never stopped loving Rosalind. And you," he declared with a boyish grin, giving my shoulders an extra squeeze, "love me."

I ignored his gloating, though I couldn't find it in me to deny the claim. Instead, I countered with, "And you?"

Without a pause, he said, "Obviously, I love you too, further complicating the issue." He said it so matter-of-factly I didn't even feel the satisfaction of having made him say it.

I followed his logic to its end and still found myself at a loss. "And Cassie fits into the scenario how?"

He shrugged. "She's only been here a few hours, but she's found her way into Philip's heart."

I narrowed my eyes. "Because apparently *his* heart wasn't spoken for when she arrived—even though he was, at the time, engaged to me." I shouldn't have been surprised, remembering how Cassie had said she'd steal Philip away from me in a moment. It was the thousand disappointing dances and hundreds of smitten swains all over again. Cassie had obviously been attracted to Philip immediately, and now that I thought about it, Philip had admired her as well. At the time, I'd been far too obsessed with Jack's pointed attentions toward Cassie and her answering flirtatiousness to care.

"She's a sterling woman," he observed, "but she lacks Rose's tenacity and passion."

"And my bullheadedness and bossiness?" I offered.

He chuckled, reaching to muss my hair affectionately before continuing. "But something about her . . ." I mentally filled in the blank: her sweetness, her gentleness, her never-ending patience. "She touched his heart where he had hidden it long ago, safe from everyone."

"It can't be as simple as that," I argued.

"No. It's only the beginning. The rest will come in time."

"It's terribly convenient," I commented, even as scenes from my girlhood replayed in my mind. "You know, Cassie has always managed Father in the way Philip responds to best—not wheedling or prodding as I would do, but sending him in the direction he should go lovingly and respectfully. She'd probably be a better match for him."

"There. You see it too," he said, waving a hand as if he'd laid it all out nicely. "Everything comes out right in the end." He turned, gathering me in his arms as if he meant to kiss me right there in that filthy closet, with spiders watching from the corners and cobwebs caught in my hair. The less-than-romantic environment might not have bothered me if it hadn't been for something else. I put up a hand, stopping him.

His eyebrows rose in silent inquiry. Surely, they seemed to say, everything was settled. The golden beauty had tamed the beast. The steward had won his maid. What more remained?

"Woo," I said simply.

"Woo?" he repeated, his face a mask of confusion.

"I recall two separate occasions when I laid my heart before you only to have it trampled. I need you to woo me, Jack. Now. Or I promise you I'll leave this closet and find a job as a maid or a cook as far away as possible."

He studied me for a moment, and seeing that I meant what I said, he withdrew his arms from around me. Turning so that he was facing the room, he folded up his long legs and rested his elbows on his knees. For a moment he looked more like a troubled boy than a man, and I fought the urge to ease the concern from his brow with assurances of my affections. But I held myself back.

He sighed. "I'm a simple man, Bella, with little to offer a woman. I was content to live on when Rose left, nursing a broken heart and believing I would never love again. I did my duty for Philip year after year and thought that would be enough. Then, when he came striding home one day, his face painted with anger and a pathetic bundle in his arms, everything changed. You captured my interest from that first moment." He agitatedly ran a hand through his hair. "I listened to you railing at Philip that night, and I admired your courage. I realized what you didn't—that you were as damaged as the rest of us, and I determined to make your life here as comfortable as possible."

Affectionately, I remembered all he had done for me: searching the forest for my things, insisting I have decent accommodations, providing fresh food from the market, drawing me baths, and most important, offering his friendship from the first moment we met.

"Watching you struggle to grow into your role, I fell in love with you. I found everything about you appealing."

"Even my feistiness?" I prodded, poking him in the shoulder with a finger.

A grin quirked his lips. "Especially that. But as my feelings for you grew, so did Philip's."

"And?"

Shrugging, he reiterated, "What did I have to offer? I knew what you wanted out of life, and Philip could provide it for you. You'd done so much for him already, helping him more in a matter of months than I had in years. I thought you would grow to love one another."

After a moment's consideration, I admitted meekly, "So did I."

At my confession, the corner of his mouth twisted grimly. "I believed I was doing what was best for both of you. I did all I could to push you together. Everything seemed a success until I realized the depth of my feelings for you. I could no longer stand idly by and watch you fall in love with my friend, especially when I knew of your feelings for me. That's when I decided to leave, to start a new life far from you and give you a chance for the type of life you always wanted."

"Would you really have gone?" I questioned, remembering how devastating the thought of never seeing him again had been.

"Yes," he said simply. "I would have taken what pride I had left and started over someplace else."

"Leaving me with a man I didn't love, even though I'd made my feelings for you clear?" I had to say it, even though I knew it would pain him.

"Yes," he admitted. "But then I saw you storm past in Rose's dress. You looked like a thundercloud ready to rain destruction on any who got in your way. And then I understood what I'd done."

Gazing ruefully down at the ruined gown, now hopelessly stained beyond repair, I asked, "You knew it was hers?"

He nodded slowly. "Seeing the dress again, I realized that Philip had never recovered from losing Rose. Some part of him still belonged to her." His eyes were wistful for a moment, but then a cockeyed grin crept into place and crinkled them at the corners. "I think you cured him of that, though—bringing it to his attention in your sweet way," he teased, settling his arm around my shoulders once again. "And you may have opened the door for your sister at the same time." He smoothed down one of my errant locks and tucked my head under his chin, letting out a sigh as he did so. "I'm sorry, Bella. I thought I was giving you the best chance at happiness. Can you ever forgive me?"

"I'll consider it," I said, nestling against him, feeling, as I always did, perfectly safe and secure in the circle of his embrace.

"Then I'll spend all my life earning your forgiveness," he vowed.

I marveled that destiny had chosen a better future for

me than what I had selected for myself. As a steward's wife, the life of serving and caring for others would be mine, but Jack would be by my side to share in the work. All the things I had devalued before—joy, happiness, love—would be within my grasp. The future unfolded before me, different than I had pictured it, but somehow brighter than I had ever imagined.

We sat that way for several minutes, curled together in the bottom of the closet, oblivious to our surroundings and content in the knowledge of our own happy ending. Then, remembering something, I pulled away far enough to half glare up at him and break the companionable silence with, "Isn't this when you're supposed to ask me to marry you, Jack? What is it with you men?" I mocked. "Are you incapable of asking a woman outright if she'll marry you?"

He chuckled again, a self-conscious grin spreading over his face. He smoothed it away, putting on a serious expression and bowing his head solemnly. "Pardon me, my lady." He moved to kneel before me.

"Mind the broken glass," I warned. "And the lamp."

"Quite," he agreed, looking down to avoid them. Carefully, he settled on the remains of the ginger gown, faced me, and took my hands in his. "Bella, will you do me the honor of becoming my wife?" he asked.

I looked at him: handsome, kind, loving, and willing to sacrifice everything for my happiness. I would never find his equal. My heart throbbed with love, but I couldn't resist. "Give up all my dreams of wealth and acclaim to be the wife of a steward?"

"Yes." He bowed his head again, his gaze dropping to the floor.

"There's nothing I'd rather do," I whispered, slipping my arms around his neck. His face alight with joy, he buried me in an embrace again. After a moment, his lips found mine, awakening a passion that had lain dormant since our last kiss. The wreckage around us receded, our world shrinking to the size of a cozy closet floor, all concern for the past and the future melting away in the brilliance of the present.

Seventeen

I scrubbed furiously at my face, trying to remove a stubborn smudge. A knock sounded at the door, and I ignored it, focused on getting that last bit of grime off my cheek. The knocking sounded again, this time more insistently.

"Be patient!" I snapped at the door. "I was covered in filth, remember? And I had to change out of that hideous dress all by myself."

"I did offer to help."

I glared at the door, irritated by the impertinence of the statement. Nervous throat clearing sounded from the other side.

"Sorry. That's not what I—"

"The process would go much more quickly if I wasn't interrupted every three seconds." Honestly, just because a girl had committed to marry a man didn't entitle him to run her life. I might as well make it clear from the beginning that I didn't plan to roll over and let Jack walk all over me just because we were engaged.

The message seemed to get through this time, for I was left in peace to finish my ablutions. The silence on the other side of the door was so absolute that I worried he'd gotten offended and stormed off. But when I opened the door a few minutes later, I found him leaning against the opposite wall with a look of meekness painted across his face. He had taken far less time than I had to clean up, his dark hair curling damply over his brow. Between the fresh smell of him and the expression on his face, my irritation faded away.

"I really didn't mean to offer to help you remove your clothing," he felt the need to clarify.

"Of course you didn't," I replied archly. "Why would a man ever want to remove a woman's clothing?" Slipping my arm through his and pulling him toward the staircase, I said, "Come on." He only shook his head, chuckled, and fell into step beside me.

Arm in arm, we reached the library, the sound of voices audible from the corridor. Jack reached for the doorknob, then paused to look back at me. "Are you sure about this?" he asked.

I nodded.

Jack twisted the knob, pulled the door open, and stepped aside so that I could enter first. Not sure what to expect after my dramatic exit earlier in the day, I scanned the room. Instead of the organized study Philip usually maintained, a number of books were scattered haphazardly about the floor, intermixed with enough paper fragments to indicate that the top of the desk had been hastily cleared, most likely in anger or frustration. Philip sat in his armchair surrounded by the mess, his back bowed and his head in his hands. He'd been in the process of saying something when we entered, and I glanced around to see who he'd been addressing. In my armchair beside the fire, carefully removed from the clutter, was Cassie, her busy knitting needles glinting in the firelight. Her keen eye ran over me in that motherly way she had, ensuring that I was safe and sound before offering up a small smile of welcome.

"Good evening, Bella. I trust all is well?" she said.

I nodded bemusedly, still taken aback by the scene I'd intruded upon.

"Philip, don't you have something to say to Bella?" she prompted. Her tone reminded me of mothers prodding naughty children to apologize for their misdeeds.

Philip cast her a sheepish glance before straightening and turning his eyes on me. He cleared his throat. "I'm sorry, Bella."

The words were simple, but I knew what they'd cost him, and in a moment I was by his side, kneeling in the mess of books and papers about his feet. Jack, tracking after me as quietly as a shadow, positioned himself behind Philip's chair. "I'm sorry too," I said quietly, slipping my hand into his and squeezing it. "It seems we were both untruthful, which would have been a very poor way to begin a marriage."

"Can you forgive me?" he asked, his brow rumpled and his gray eyes remorseful.

"If you promise to forgive yourself and move on with your life." It was all I wanted for him.

He cast another look at Cassie, and she smiled encouragingly back at him. I wondered if he knew how many men would have happily surrendered their lands, titles, and the bulk of their holdings to be on the receiving end of that smile. "We were just speaking of that," he said. "And I'm going to do my best."

"Then you have my ready forgiveness." I squeezed his hand again and grinned up at him. "Now that's settled, I wish to speak to you of something else." In a moment, Jack was at my elbow, helping me to my feet. Sliding an arm around his waist, I stood at his side. Together, we faced Philip.

Philip's eyes narrowed as he took in the sight of us. He turned a glare on Cassie. "Did you know about this?" he demanded.

She didn't reply, but she did raise an admonitory eyebrow. It was enough to quell him. "Sorry," he muttered. Then he turned back to face us. "It seems my steward has fallen in love with my fiancée," he said. "Again."

Jack's arm tightened around me reassuringly. "To be precise," he replied, "this time I fell in love with your scullery maid."

Philip chuckled self-deprecatingly. "How could I be so blind?" He glanced once more at Cassie. "You knew, didn't you?" She offered no reply other than an enigmatic half shrug. He shook his head in disbelief. "Right under my nose, and I missed it."

I saw my in and seized it. "That's what we wanted to speak to you about, Philip. Everything has become too complicated. With so many people coming and going all the time, it's practically impossible to find time to think about things. However, Jack and I have come up with a solution."

His eyes, already stormy, turned a shade more sorrowful. "You're leaving?" he said, his voice breaking on the last word.

"No," I hurried to explain. "We're staying. There's nothing we'd like more." Jack squeezed my waist in encouragement. "But what if we let some of the staff go? Not everyone, mind you." I thought of Penelope, Suzy, and James, the arrogant butler, who had practically become permanent fixtures in their brief time here. "Only some of them."

"We also discussed putting a damper on the plans for renovation," Jack added, "just for the time being."

Philip regarded his friend thoughtfully. "You always did prefer the simple life, Jack. Even when we were children."

Jack smirked, making no argument.

"But I'm surprised to hear this from you, Bella. Isn't living in the lap of luxury what you always wanted?"

"One's tastes do change," I said, beaming up at Jack.

Philip released a sigh of forbearance. "What do you think, Cassandra?" he asked, deferring to my sister, whom he had known less than a day.

Dear Cassie, I thought, *charming to the core.*

She set down her knitting and met his gaze, her eyes crinkling with delight as she said, "It's a wonderful idea. I'd love to be a part of it."

"Nothing would give me more pleasure," Philip replied, his eyes full of adoration. With an effort, he refocused on Jack and me. "Very well," he said in a businesslike tone.

"As it seems I am outnumbered, I will do as you wish. Under one condition."

"Yes?" I asked, wondering what request he would make.

"I will do the gardening."

By morning, I was back at my post in the kitchen, dusting the flour off my hands as I set the dough to rise. Philip had refused to let go of the cook, but I was equally determined that Jack should have his fresh bread each morning. So I ignored the cook's sour looks and grumbling and kept my hands busy. Before long, even she admitted I had a knack for it.

Cassie assumed the role of housekeeper with a relish I couldn't have anticipated. It was easy to picture her running the household permanently. Perhaps, in her own quiet way, she enjoyed ordering others about as much as I did.

Philip established his place in the garden, dismissing all the gardeners except a young man from the village named Jonas. Together, they did as well as the horde of gardeners had ever done. Whenever Philip became angry or frustrated, he'd retreat to his beloved rose bed, muttering incoherently to Jonas or the plants and weeding with a fury I'd not witnessed since before we cut his hair. Neither the plants nor Jonas seemed to be bothered by this, and in time, Philip returned to good spirits.

My father and Aaron were also eager to help out, each taking on the tasks they enjoyed most. This meant that they often helped Jack with household repairs or could be found tinkering in the stable and imagining new inventions to make our lives easier.

My father and Philip were alike in so many ways that they naturally found occasion both during the daytime and in the evening, after we retired to the study, to discuss and debate various topics. Seeing them interact reminded me that Philip's own father had passed away while he was still young, before the crisis of Rose's disappearance had occurred, and that Philip had had no one but Jack to see him through it. In time, my father fell into the role of mentor, managing Philip as he did his own children—with kindness and patience.

In spite of my father's and Cassie's influences, Philip didn't transform into Prince Charming. He always retained a certain amount of surliness, which I found comforting. It was a more truthful representation of his character—not as sweet as he had once been with Rose or as craggy as he had been with me, but somewhere in between, with characteristics of both the young man and the Beast.

"My, aren't we the industrious bunch?" Philip commented as he watched Cassie and I hard at work in the kitchen and my father and Aaron—visible through the window—aiding Jack in expanding the stable.

Cassie corrected him gently, "Not a *bunch*, Philip. A family." She smiled warmly. "The way we rely on each other and help one another can only be described as family."

The habitually pensive look he'd had since childhood settled onto his face, his gray eyes sober as he digested this comment. After a moment, a slight curve lifted up one side of his mouth.

A family, I thought. As I watched my future husband work alongside my father and brother, a feeling of warmth settled in my chest. For the first time in my life, I understood what it truly meant.

Father was waiting for us at the bottom of the stairs. His eyes lit up when he saw his daughters, dressed more beautifully than ever before, descending to meet him. He greeted us each with a kiss, then hustled me onward and settled Cassie onto his arm. Casting them a backward glance, I saw a look of love, pride, and the heart's best wishes pass between them before I hurried out the open front doors. A lump formed in my throat, and my vision grew hazy with happy tears.

"Everything all right?" Jack caught my hand as I stepped out the door.

I nodded in reply, slowing to a comfortable ramble as we made our way across the lawn to a secluded grove of trees a short distance away. He looked at me approvingly out of the corner of his eye, "You look as lovely as a bride, Bella," he said warmly, leaning in to kiss my cheek.

"The last time I looked as lovely as a bride, I was covered in dust, grime, and an unimaginable amount of tears," I replied, arching a brow up at him, "so you'll pardon me if I don't return the compliment."

He laughed aloud, the sound ringing out, full and carefree. "Lovely even then," he pronounced, lifting my hand to his lips. I wanted to roll my eyes at the obvious lie, but I couldn't stop the flutter in my stomach when his lips brushed the back of my hand, and I grinned up at him instead.

Fragments of music and voices bent in polite conversation lilted over the lawn. We followed them to their source, a secluded clearing near the manor. Once inside, I paused in amazement, taken by the sheer beauty of the place. The circle of trees was garlanded with strands of flowers trailing white ribbons. In the center of the grove stood a small arbor adorned with numberless pastel-hued rose blossoms.

Jack turned to look at me, trying to read my expression. "What do you think?" he asked.

The arbor, I knew, and much of the decoration, had been arranged at his direction. "It's perfect," I replied, seeing his face brighten at my approval. He had wanted more than anything for this day to be just right.

My gaze fell on Philip, who was standing before the arbor, white as a sheet and wringing his hands in a most uncharacteristic fashion. I looked up at Jack imploringly. Understanding, he released my hands and urged me forward.

Hurrying across the grove, I took Philip's hands in mine and found them unaccountably cool. "Cold feet?" I teased.

He huffed out half a laugh, his face falling back into grim lines afterward. "I wish," he confided. "I'm simply terrified."

I smiled knowingly up at him and said, "That's as it should be. You were never terrified with me." I squeezed his hands, trying my best to tease him into good humor. "And you should have been. Life with me would have been a living terror. I'd have made sure of it."

My efforts at easing his tension were rewarded with an actual chuckle, and his gloomy expression lightened somewhat. "Will you ever forgive me, Bella?" It was a question he'd asked countless times, but no matter how many times I reassured him that I already had, it continued to haunt him. The whole of it was written plainly in his grave eyes. Yet when I had come to him on the arm of his best friend, dressed in Rosalind's tattered wedding gown, he had readily and humbly forgiven me.

"Just make her happy, Philip," I said simply, "and I promise to forgive all past and future mistakes."

His stormy eyes were bright with unshed tears. "I'll do my best," he promised.

"That's good enough for me," I said, turning to leave him. But he grabbed my hand and pulled me back.

"I almost forgot," he said, patting down his pockets frantically. The panic in his eyes eased as he found what he sought. "I believe this is yours." He pressed the ruby pendant into my palm.

I stared at it for a moment, watching it glint in my palm. "This belongs to Cassie."

He wrapped my fingers closed around it. "No. It will always be yours, Bella. None of this would've happened without you."

At that moment, the music paused, and Philip glanced up. Catching sight of a lithe figure making its way toward him through the trees, his breath caught. I moved to his side to watch Cassandra's progress across the grove.

"Will I ever be worthy of her?" he whispered, the words laced with doubt.

"Does it matter?" I asked, turning to smile up at him. "She loves you just as you are."

Jack was once again at my side, his fingers intertwined with mine. He commented, "I've never seen a more beautiful bride." Cassie, in the shimmering dress Father had given her what felt like ages ago, drifted across the clearing on Father's arm to clasp hands with Philip. Cassie's beauty shone out like a beacon, her golden hair gleaming in the summer sunlight, her dress perfectly outlining the curves of her slim form. The jewels she wore winked in the late afternoon light, though her eyes beamed more brilliantly than the sapphires she wore as she gazed up at her husband-to-be.

With one hand, I squeezed Jack's hand, and with the other, I pressed the ruby to my heart. In my mind, another wedding unfolded. It was a plain affair, taking place in a room no fancier than my home had been and attended by no more than the simply dressed couple and the minister. The groom, a nervous redhead, glanced up at his beautiful dark-haired bride. "Are you sure? You could have had anything you wanted."

She smiled up at him, her cheeks dimpling. Even in a plain, white, muslin dress without adornment, she was lovely. "I want you, Jamie."

Hope brightened his expression, but he still asked, "Won't it bother you to be a farmer's wife, Rosie?"

Taking his hand in hers, she said, "It's a dream come true."

Jack spoke, the vision fading at his words. "Can you

really wait? Even at my best, I could never provide this for you."

"I don't care," I said, thinking of Rose and the love shining in her eyes during her simple wedding ceremony. I squeezed the jewel, my connection to her. "If you wanted to get married right here and now, I'd say yes."

His brows lifted eagerly.

"No." I shook my head dismissively. "This is their day. Let them have it. Ours will come soon enough."

A modest home of our own, a wedding ring, and something set aside to live on—Jack was determined to provide me with at least these before we took our vows. Philip had generously offered us the cottage Jack's parents had once inhabited, located near the great stone house, but that was all Jack had allowed him to do. It was a point of pride for Jack to provide what he could for his bride, and I agreed, preferring to pool what little resources we had to renovate and refurbish the small building over accepting charity. For the first time in my life, I was content to do without the luxuries that were being showered on my sister—just for the pleasure of having Jack by my side.

"Are you sure?" he asked intently, the question bringing Rose and Jamie to mind.

I leaned up to kiss him softly on the lips and whispered, "It's a dream come true."

Author's Note

*O*nce upon a time, there was a little princess. Or at least, obsessed as she was with an illustration of Beauty poised before a mirror, a magical comb twining each golden curl into the perfect coiffure, she longed to be a princess.

She grew older, as all would-be princesses do, and certain details of the fairy tale left her dissatisfied. The young princess's first love, the delightfully animalistic Beast, who is two inches away from leaving the nearby village decimated one minute and beautifully softened by his affection for Beauty the next, epitomized the real magic of the tale: the power of love. But when the Beast transforms physically—his beastliness replaced with courtly manners and perfect good looks—no matter what the rendition, how beautiful executed the illustrations, or how gentlemanly the prince, the young princess always missed the Beast.

And Beauty? Throughout her life, the princess, growing wiser, encountered many a true beauty. Unlike the Beauty of the tale, with her infallible good looks and self-sacrificing nature, those beauties lost patience with their overly energetic offspring and left dirty dishes in the sink if there was a *Pride and Prejudice* marathon on. As a woman undermined on the path to perfection by her own sarcastic sense of humor and quick temper, the grown-up princess both admired the traditional Beauty and longed to smack her soundly.

That was how Bella was born. She is the Beauty for those who, like our princess, aspire to perfection but are hindered by their own humanity. Bella, brilliant and ruthless, weaves a tale that fills the void left by those before it—at least for this princess.

Acknowledgments

ecoming Beauty having its day in the sun instead of lurking in the nether reaches of my hard drive is due to a number of wonderful people. First off, I want to thank the editors (Alissa, Melissa, and Daniel), designers, and other professionals at Cedar Fort for capturing my vision in both cover art and prose form. A big thanks to the Cedar Fort team for making me look good!

And Misty, Cindy, Jo, Melissa, and Amy, thank you for refusing to take no for an answer and for believing in Bella and me when I wasn't sure we were fit to be seen in public. You're the best writerly friends a girl can have!

Thanks also to family and friends for tolerating everything from "Does this sound stupid?" to big girl tizzie fits. I never would have made it here without your love and support.

Lastly, a big thank you to my readers for giving a fairy tale obsessed newbie a chance. Lots of love to you all!

Discussion Questions

1. BELLA'S FATHER IS a single parent who freely sacrifices whatever is needed for his family—even ungrateful Bella. Could his behavior toward his children be considered overly indulgent? Is this ultimately helpful or harmful? How might life have been different if his wife had survived?

2. CASSANDRA'S GOODNESS, BEAUTY, and seeming good fortune grate on Bella's nerves, until she discovers that her sister has been struggling with her own challenges all her life. Have you known someone (real or fictional) who is irritatingly good, beautiful, or moral, but might be hiding some secret heartache or challenge? How would knowing this change your perception of them?

3. IN AN ATTEMPT to achieve her full potential, Rosalind abandons everyone and everything she has ever known. Bella too considers leaving her loved ones

behind in pursuit of a more purposeful life. Is this an act of bravery or cowardice?

4. LOVE LOST IS a recurring theme in *Becoming Beauty*. Compare the different ways that Bella's father, Philip, and Jack cope with the loss of loved ones. Is there a healthy way to deal with the crippling effects of grief?

5. TRADITIONALLY, BEAUTY AND the Beast is a tale about the power of a change of heart. Bella, like the Beast in the traditional tale, experiences a change of heart, questions her basic beliefs and life choices, and ultimately becomes a better person. Discuss real world examples of individuals who have succeeded in changing their situations in life. What inspired them to do so?

6. SEVERAL EXAMPLES OF romantic love are represented in the novel. Compare Bella's father's example of lasting love for and dedication to his wife, Cassie falling in love with Philip at first sight and working to build a relationship with him, and Bella's friendship with Jack that slowly turns into love. What is required to build a lasting relationship?

About the Author

Sarah E. Boucher spends her days instilling young children with the same love of literature she has known since childhood. After hours, she pens her own stories and nurses an unhealthy obsession for handbags, high heels, baking, and British television. Sarah is a graduate of Brigham Young University. She lives and teaches in Ogden, Utah. *Becoming Beauty* is her first novel. Contact Sarah by email, or on Twitter, Pinterest, Facebook, or Instagram by visiting her website at saraheboucher.com.